Jane and
Will Soon

by

ERNA BRODBER

NEW BEACON BOOKS

LONDON : PORT OF SPAIN

First published 1980
by New Beacon Books Ltd.,
76 Stroud Green Road, London N4 3EN, England.

© 1980 Erna Brodber

ISBN 901241 36 9 hardback
      901241 37 7 paperback

Reprinted 1988
Reprinted 1993

Printed by Villiers Publications Ltd
26a Shepherds Hill, London N6 5AH

Contents

MY DEAR
WILL YOU ALLOW ME

VOICES

One

Papa's grandfather and Mama's mother were the upper reaches of our world. So we were brown, intellectual, better and apart, two generations of lightening blue-blacks and gracing elementary schools with brightness. The cream of the earth, isolated, quadroon, mulatto, Anglican. But we had two wiry black hands up to the elbows in khaki suds, cleanly singing:

-Brother Jack, we must get the sugar out if we are to supply the cakes-

-Too true, Miss Tucker, too true -forever organising . . . people, corn, cane, cow, tired but happily sure of a Baptist seat in Heaven.

-Cock-fighting on a Sunday! Lord take the case.-

It is hard work that gets a Baptist Amen through lips pursed for the Te Deum.

-Mother says I must stop writing to you-

-All right, but you must write to let me know why she says so-

-She says all this writing is not good for me for I must take my Training College exams-

-But she must know that writing is good practice for your exams. Tell her I say so-

-She says no good can come out of you-

-Show her the pillow cases I bought you-

-She says you haven't made your intentions clear-

-Show her the ring-

7

-She says you are ten years older than I and you have nothing to show for it-

-Let her see your waist-

Yes now. The chile life spoil. Lord take the case! Those sneaking khaki lips forcing poor little Baptist contractions. Not only one time, but twice, five times, six times. Oh God. Poor chile. But she must have out her lot.

-I got a scholarship Granny-

-That's what my father said, "Your blessings shall flow like a river. Not unto your children but to your children's children"-

-The best one Granny-

-Praise to the Redeemer. Paul may sow and Apollos may water but the increase come from God. Learn that Nellie and quiet yourself-

Quiet yourself Nellie. You had nothing to do with it or anything else. Your Granny Tucker proposes and God disposes. He is the God of creation and who is you?

Two

It was not for nothing that Vivian Virtue called our part of the universe 'mossy coverts, dim and cool'. We lived in a mossy covert, dim and cool and very dark. And we could make it darker still when we played dolly house in our sink hole searching for treasures which the sea washed up or when we stared into the irridescent black ink that made our dark night. Our moon-lights you would love: nothing can beat moonlight upon oceans of banana leaves . . . banana leaves shifting their shoulders like rag effigies of our politicians. Banana leaves, now the dying swan, now the chorus of the Les Sylphides, dancing with quiet, controlled conviction. Like ours. We had just sung:

> -There is a lovely island in the Caribbean Sea
> An island full of coconuts and fine banana trees
> An island where the sugar cane is waving in the
>   breeze
> Jamaica is its name.
> We are out to build a new Jamaica. . . .-

In four parts, full and strong and with conviction that having sung, there would be no more leaf spot, that there would be no more soil erosion and that we had built anew.

Ever see a fowl sitting on eggs in cold December rain. We knew the warmth and security of those eggs in the dark of her bottom.

No. You'll find no finger posts to point you to our place. The stone at our gate says 29 but it doesn't say to where. For all we know or care, it is a tombstone like the one at church that covers white people's spirits. Yes. It is difficult to find us. Mountains ring us round and cover us, banana leaves shelter us and sustain us, boiled, chips, porridge, three times a day. You should see the poor insipid sun trying to penetrate us! You had to help him on. You had to go for him and pull his hand, crawling behind you even then in a long shadow. It had to be twelve o'clock before he could catch up with you. Poor insipid sun. Fighting the banana leaves to come in. Muted strength. Not even enough to take clothes off the line. Muted tone.

In muted tones outside came in. A pink parson, insipid as the sun. A song: 'Mospan, Two Gun Rhygin'; The newspaper headlines: Match factory on strike . . . Headless corpse found. Some nonsense words for our games: The Colon Secretary. I will play the Colon Secretary. Who know why the private salute with four fingers and the officer with three? I know . . . I know . . . Everybody know that. The private say "I'm your dog Sir" and the officer say "Yes I know it".

Outside infiltrated our nest only as its weave allowed.

Three

Dearie : You see this pillar gate. A white lady used to live here name Miss Ann and when she married, red carpet spread from here go clear round church. She did own the whole of this place and before she dead, she walk round the whole district begging salt in a cal'bash bowl.

Sister : Like Mass Tanny

Dearie : Leave out Mass Tanny; he living. But you see over Church, the big tomb. Her son bury in it and it mark 1856. He was a drunk-aready.

Sister : Is only stone. Nothing don't bury in it. He die at sea. Is a monument. We don't 'fraid for him.

Dearie : No. We don't 'fraid for him. Is only stone.

Sister : But Mass Tanny now. . . .

Dearie : How much time I must tell you . . . don't call him name.

You see Mass Tanny walking in the water table and smiling. Just you smile at him when he smiles at you and be polite to him. Don't say anything about him. He is Dearie's uncle and Sweet Boy's grandfather and Girlie who works with us, her mother used to be his wife. You didn't know. Well you know now. Everybody is related here and people can turn your head behind you. Mind how you talk. Bush have ears. And remember, don't eat anything from him or anybody else outside of this yard unless you let me see it. You hear. You hear me Nellie and Sister. You must be careful.

Sweet Boy : You know that Mass Stanley did have a sister what pass first year and pickney carry poison egg and give her at school and she dead ! Her hair drop off clean clean before she dead.

Girlie : And you see Mass Cliff that silent mad. Him did

bright bright you know and is people do him so.

Lawks. People wicked eh!

A boil is a raising on the skin. Don't squeeze the head. It will never give 'til the root is ready to come out. Dearie and Sister, Sweet Boy and Girlie and all of us mouth; the voice belongs to the family group dead and alive. We walk by their leave, for planted in the soil, we must walk over them to get where we are going.

Mass Nega, beg you mine yourself. Mi smell you dinner but mi no want none.

Our dead and living had no stone encasements. Miss Ann and her son Charlie are tombed and harmless. Our dead and living are shrouded together under zinc, sweet potato slips and thatch. Step warily. One body raises itself into a mountain of bodies which overtop to form a pit or a shelter for you.

Four

What was it for Dotty? A pit or a shelter. For an eight year old girl foaming upon a grave.

Mass Less re-incarnated knocked the poor chile out at recess time and entered her, dear Jesus to sing the praises of a long dead four-eye man. An eight year old child wake up with the face of her sixty year old grand-uncle to sell fortunes three pence a piece, to kill cock, bathe big ole man and say prayer ! Poor chile.

But they should a did tell her not to play on the ole man's grave and they should a did hear him when him say that him want rice and fowl. Now he can't even dead for a man have three score years and ten and poor Dotty only eight. And it could a did happen to you.

My father spoke too from the depths of his family pit or shelter. We all had them. We spoke of Dorcas. At New Year's eve our clan gathers never tired of tears and never weary of the warmth of sadness.

My father : Another New Year's eve like this, the bigger ones of us went to church. We had left every one at home hearty.

Us : What is hearty? (Someone asked every year.)

My father : Well. Very well. For only that evening Dorcas has said "Mummah, the gungo peas is fit. Let me shell it for dinner". She was the most beautiful of us . . . smooth-skinned, fair with straight pretty hair and she was to go to school in January.

Us (We urged every year) : So what happened?

My father : We hear some people saying that Mrs Richmond daughter poorly and the whole family sick but we couldn't believe. We go home to find the five little ones, Uncle Jo-Jo, Uncle Lester, Mag, all of them sick and poor little Dorcas dead.

Us : But what kill her?

My father : We will never know. But it must be what they call now the vomiting sickness . . . the black boil then or something somebody set. We don't know.

Once a year Aunt Dorcas sat with us in person. Uncle Lester too occasionally. He it was who took the death of Aunt Becca. (We know that for Mass Tanny was confessing.)

Life is scary when you talk about it. But is not me one frighten. Everybody else frighten too and they quiet, quiet, when my father stop talking. Is a funny thing but when the people you close to 'fraid, is a warm fear. And you feel that if you stay close to them, the bad spirit will pass. So you step warily, follow your elders' words and let them take your hand.

Is not we one 'fraid.

Next door at Mass Stanley, they frighten too. Frighten at what we might do. And they're doing the same thing . . . stepping warily and taking their elders' hands. We are families walking bravely in fear, secure in family fear. Each praising God that we live to see another New Year's morning come.

Five

Mass Mehiah is cutting down his bastard cedar trees. Knock, knock. You hear it. He is making a new meeting house and the American bishop is going to open it. Brrrrrrrrrrrh. Brrrrrrrrrrrh. You hear it! Strange voices floating in through bamboo poles, carrying news of outside . . . Test Match, train crash . . . into drawing rooms and kitchens. The sun is walking bravely now and has cracked my neighbour's calabash. While he turns his back to fix it, we'll ship this one out with the evening sun. Go eena kumbla.

Go eena kumbla
-Go eena kumbla- Brer Anancy begged his son Tucuma.
-Go eena kumbla- Polonius advised.
-Go eena kumbla lest Dry Head eat you-
Mr and Mrs Anancy for all their cunning can spare me nothing more towards my migration than

-Go eena kumbla-

Six

-You remember Baba Ruddock, Auntie-

-No-

-You must remember him. He's from our place-

-If you say I must, then I suppose I must-

-You must remember him. Mass Stanley's grandson. You know Mass Stanley, Auntie. He used to be the best quadrille dancer and you yourself said that he used to be the best jitterbug dancer when you were young. Yes Auntie, you remember Baba. He used to recite well. But he never did come to our Sunday School so perhaps you really don't remember him. But all the same you would be proud of him. If you see him! Going up for prizes so often. History prize, Maths prize and with all that, deputy head boy and captain of the cricket team. You would be proud.-

-Hmm-

-He is the most popular boy at school and he wants to take me to see Jack the Ripper.-

Silence

-You know the film that is showing at the Globe-

Silence

-But Globe is just around the corner. Nothing can happen to us-

Sigh

-But it is a Saturday night and I am on holidays-

-It is my responsibility-

-But I am sixteen, a prefect at school and a patrol leader. You let me go on hikes. You let me go to evensong and speech festival by myself at night. I don't understand-

-It is my responsibility and girls so hard to grow up-

Silence

-Somebody should tell you that his uncle spoil your Cousin B's life. Those people will drag you down child-

Silence

16

-I know you're vex but think of me. What would I tell your parents if your life get stopped part way. You have a chance to make something of your life. Seize it-

-But Globe is just around the corner. What could happen in that little space of time?-

-Hmm. Somebody should tell you that it only takes two seconds . . . that you would have to go back to that place and sit down on your mother and your father-

-So I must sit here quiet like an alabaster baby because I am my cousin B?-

-Learn that lest you be weighed in the balance and found wanting. Learn that the world is waiting to drag you down. "Woman luck de a dungle heap", they say, "fowl come scratch it up". But you save yourself lest you turn woman before your time, before the wrong fowl scratch your luck-

God slackens the weave. Separates us chicken from birds. Sends us to pick our way through crowded buses, electric wire and asphalt streets yet gives us no street map towards each other. No compass, no scale either. Leaves us no path, no through way, no gap in our circle.

And His will be done. You must be right Aunt Becca. You have to be so careful of those people.

THE TALE OF THE SNAIL IN THE KUMBLA

One

But when you live on a compound with eight hundred men and women, they press you, Auntie. Everywhere; trying to spoil your life. What can you do? Stick to the girls so nothing will happen? Make men your brothers, be on the front line of clubs and societies, read? The compound is naked and unashamed; the moon is dropping anytime. God is calling Auntie. Any girl would want to see it. And they say you won't see much without a man.

-She ain't got a man?-

-You must be joking-

-Ah going mek a press-

-So you don't understand the renaissance. Let's see. But you can dance! Imagine that. And you like to walk! Now look at that. We are going to see the renaissance.

-You have to admit I've been patient. Three years and you've used every trick in the book. Look at you now. Eating grass with the moon about to mount the earth. You are purposely hanging back. What's with you. Hurry up.— You'll miss the moment.

-You can't help it. OK. I know. I've been pressing you too hard. I'll wait. It's going to be all right. You'll see.

-My God how you shudder. It is me. You are afraid of me. You are repulsed by me. After all these years. Dancing but you haven't moved a foot. You are safe my girl. Don't worry. Keep spinning your circles dear; but you'll see the day when you bind your feet so close that you will trip at your own pirouette.-

-The man swallow his pride and ask me to talk to you. You don't know why. Is hard you hard so or is feelings you don't have. You really don't know why? Poor boy! No point talking to you. You not real. Poor Boy. Hitting his head against a blasted fortress. You really not real. They have no right letting you out 'mongst people. Is not so much that you don't understand as that you 'fraid to feel.-

Saved Auntie. Keep them off. Lest you be weighed in the balance and found wanting.

Is there no way out?
No gap in this circle?
What a hell of a scream! Is there no way out Saviour Divine? Let me try to hold it in. But I'm going to vomit and the world is spinning on its axle 66.6 degrees. Vomit up a scream. The walls are moving in and somebody is holding my throat. Good. That will help. So nobody will know she can't hold a man. Let go my throat. Gas is suffocating me. It is the transfiguration. Will I ascend. I'm spinning, I'm so giddy, so light. Weighed in the balance and found wanting. But what have I done to be buried alive. I've tried to be good. Yes. My man has died, but I am falling; against the church. It's all right. Calm, quiet now. Let the electrodes of that brick wall activate every cell in your cranium: Works without faith is not enough. Not enough. That's what he has to give and wants me to call him father. Holy Father! You are mad. Walking up and down the asphalt road in your high-heeled shoes. You are mad. Stay off the compound. They will say you are mad

19

and cannot hold a man. The sun will melt the brick that is in your brain and return it to normal functioning. "A bunch of red roses please". Walking down the road with a bunch of red roses in my high-heeled shoes. The prickles will jab your fingers: and the running blood will make you normal. Walking down the asphalt road in my high-heeled shoes and the hot sun with a bunch of red roses. Duck. People will say you are mad, like Miss Mal. People will call you Malvina Psalms. Drake stole her man but who's got mine. Best leave this place altogether.

Two

How did it begin?

Was it in the cool yellow summer when nobody troubled you and you troubled nobody. They didn't even call you to eat. You just ate and played and sewed and dreamed all at your own pace. Nobody even bothered the mango trees; they dropped at their own pace which happily was yours. In step with you and the yellow canes stripped themselves clean of their prickly sand and said "I'm ready, eat me". Natural co-operation. Even government too. So there is no nine o'clock bell to bother you and you don't bother your mother either. No need to say "Who put that there?", "Whose foot mark that?" for you are out of the house and the grass says: "It's OK roll on me". So you roll. And the jealous trench says: "See I too am dry. Roll in me". So you roll, feet clenched round your partner's neck, feet wrapped round yours. You are one. And you roll and roll gathering no moss and you drop in a trench. Plups. And you push and you push up the trench side. Skill man. Then you roll and roll and roll.

My father is a farmer and he believes in God. Paul may sow and Apollos may water but the increase comes from God. So he plants in winter and he mulches in spring but the summer belongs to God, to rest and a little travel. Everybody has changed to give God his time. My father is travelling when he should have been spraying; we are playing when we would have been working on problems of Simple Interest. But Egbert has changed in a funny way.

-The boys can hug and roll with me but you Nellie, don't let your father see you doing that with me. I don't able him come talk to me-

21

That don't make sense! When since! So you try again. Push your foot between his legs, fall him; then drop 'pon top of him and shovel him with your feet about his shoulder. Let him fight. That's what you want. That's what it is about. Bend him, curl him, push him until you win. And you win but with a difference.

No sunshine smile and "you strong though" or "let we start again". The boy get up, withdraw himself; he's not playing again and worse of all not ever again if you are there. What kind of coldness in this hot sun though. But Papa would know and he can put it together again.

Only one bus plies in our part. War Time. A blustering giant screeching 'round the bend, kicking up dust everywhere as the driver milks the piece of black tubing that is the horn. We play that game every evening. He comes groaning and shouting down Bridge Hill and we fling our feet through loose stones and marl to stand on the banking and wave. This evening we have the power for he must stop to let off our father.

-Good evening to you sir- our father is saying, -Thank you and the Lord for guiding us home safely. May He be with you on the rest of the journey -our father is saying He only talks like this at church and at meetings so this must be an adult occasion too. Or so we perceive it and this heightens our sense of ceremony. We applaud his performance and are proud of him. But we have our part too. Only for us has the bus stopped and only our father has been called upon to give this kind of speech. It is we who have the right to peep into the bus at all the gadgets (no touching of course). It is we who have a right to certain topics of conversation; it is we who have a right to talk for weeks:

You did see the horn though? No you never see

22

no horn. Me did right up into the front and me did see it. Me did see when him lift up him foot and touch it. Untruth. Bey. You never see no horn. Horn is something in him hand. Of course me did see't. You have my eye. You can tell me what I did see.

You have no friends that time. This is a family occasion. A time for family pride. Girlie and Sweet Boy and Dearie understand and they stand back. They recognise that this is your day. They leave you to the joys of cacksion, wangla and other sharings. You are in the bosom of your family. One solid phalanx. But Papa looks at me from head to toe, focuses on my middle and says with strange solemnity : -My. But you have shot up-

And my balloon stinks with shame. Something breaks and there is no warmth no more. So I am different. Something is wrong with me.

And they continue to plug holes in your sun. An egg hole a rat makes, oozing slimy yellow around your nest. Building a strange raw-smelling barrier around your private world. To touch is to contaminate.

My mother, in her dead-pan voice that I cannot figure calls out to me. It is not her scolding voice, it is not her praising voice. So what is it. No eye contact and she is pretending to sew. My God. I'm hardly eleven. What shame have you to hide from me?

Silence

-You are eleven now and soon something strange will happen to you-

Silence; still no eye contact.

-Well when it does, make sure you tell your aunt-

Period. End of sentence. I presume I am dismissed.

23

Finished. Best to forget all this strangeness but Lord, it's eating up the world.

Barry a rock n' roll ace don't want to wheel and spin no more but bend your spine like the music have no meaning and Errol can't talk straight no more. Is "x and y like me and you are two o' we" and giggles from a boy who could scrape runs out of a widow's barrel, now glassy eyed, he wants to know if they are real.

What kind of foolishness is this. And boys you know good good shouting: -Hey you can fry now- like say you don't have name no more. And your best friend telling you to pull them up, hold your back straight. Don't let boys get near to you for they can tell just by looking at your finger nails that you have it.

What a weight!
Slowly it adds up.
This bounty. Put it under a bushel or else it will shame you.

Three

Like your straw bag, Aunt Becca.

It never was mine. I could never have made it mine. For that would have been to sin. It was the most beautiful bag you've ever seen. Red and green butterflies sewn in raffia everywhere, even on the strap. And the strap; just what I had prayed for. Long; so that I could put it over my head to fall diagonally across my chest and over to the other side. A perfect gift. A wish perfectly fulfilled but I don't want to wear it and certainly not across my chest and diagonally to the side as I would have wanted.

I remember it well. It was of yellow leghorn straw and matched perfectly the yellow organdy dress that was on my bed in yellow tissue paper on the Easter Sunday of my eighth year. How come yellow at Easter? Well I am April born you see . . . the Saturday before Easter. And this year, by a strange coincidence for this only happens every six years, I hear, and I was going to be eight, my birthday was to fall on the very day on which I was born. I prayed for that bag. There was no point in praying for an Easter dress and a birthday dress. Two dresses on two consecutive days was outside of the realms of reality (though of course it was my due). They would say as they always said when they disappointed me — "The heart is willing but the flesh is weak". The handbag it would have to be then. I prayed Oh Lord I prayed. On this bag lay my claims to social identity. I prayed.

Without prodding two dresses came; a yellow tissue paper parcel and a white tissue paper parcel. An Easter dress and a birthday dress. White shoes and socks to match white Easter dress (You'd have to wear the old jippi-jappa with it but you expected that and thanked God for the new shoes and socks; only the new dress was your right). But an extra shoe box with black patent shoes and a paperbag with yellow socks to wear with the yellow puffed sleeve organdy dress and a yellow leghorn hat with a green come-follow-me. My God. What have I done. This is a day without compare.

Then Aunt Becca remembered me and sent the yellow leghorn straw bag with the green and red butterflies sewn all over it in raffia and a long strap to wear it across my chest and diagonally to the other side. It must have taken her months to make and to make it in secret! For not a rumour of the bag had reached my ear.

Right after Easter Sunday dinner the parcel came. A yellow leghorn straw bag with butterflies sewn all over it in raffia and a long strap so that it could fall diagonally and across my chest and to the other side and I was not even her favourite niece. Everybody was watching me as if to say "Now little kitten, eat and be choked". I was alone here and would be even more so at the Cantata. Me one with two dresses at Easter! Aunt Becca's bag would be my crowning shame. No one would speak to me and I would forget my lines. I refused to wear it but they wouldn't listen to me. How dare I when so many sacrifices had been made, was what they said.

And I forgot my lines Aunt Becca as you knew I would.

Aunt Becca did you send that bag to shame me, to whittle down my world, to stop me from enjoying it?

26

Four

-To make use of this bounty you got to be foreign. Right-
  -Sight-
  -Who use the beach? Who know the hills?-
  -Seen-
  -Who use your mother china bowl?-
  -Stranger-
  -Who use the crystal glasses?-
  -Still waiting for the queen-
  -Who sit in Granny's parlour-
  -Mr How-di-sah-
  -Then why you still nagging me 'bout that bow-legged
man?-
  -But he ain't come from yonder Sis. He just live down the
road-
  -You don't sight the play brother. Let me show you one
more time-

Watch the scene. A piece of nylon fog suffocatingly dry
settling over the housing scheme. See't. She is excited. Here
is a chance to experience what everybody else has experienced, a foreign country where everybody else has studied;
a foreign land. Shrouded, yet overt justification for her
isolation. You see't. She is walking home from classes,
free at last, through the streets with a mop in her hand.
No need to disguise it, no need to wrap it up. I am in a
foreign country. I live like all foreign students in a dingy,
dirty flat and I must clean it. It is the liberty of foreign
students to be strange so walk through the streets with a
mop. The script was writing itself. Sweater blouse, jeans,
cigarette puffing, part of the props even a quarrel with the
land-lady. Just right. Foreign students who wear sweater
blouses and jeans, smoke and quarrel with their land-ladies
and who live in dingy flats are permitted to be lonely.

27

They welcome male company. Enter the male. No need to be discriminating: all the play calls for is a male. He made his way across, propelling his pelvis by his bow legs. She, leaning, puffing on a column in the library or sitting under a tree or in any other such place:

He: Everyone says you've changed but I'd know you anywhere.

She: Really (eyes falsely bright).

He: How about a movie?

She: Tonight if you want.

He: Not tonight. My girl you know . . . have to take my girl friend out.

She (thinks): Loyal to his girl! Even better.

A dark movie house and his hands going where nobody else's have been. And you ought to have kicked this man out of your room, coming back on all sorts of transparent pretexts. You ought to have torn up the script and backed out. But he paid the taximan what you knew must have been his week's food, so you let him touch you. Shame. You feel shame and you see your mother's face and you hear her scream and you feel the snail what she see making for your mouth. One long nasty snail, curling up, straightening out to show its white underside that the sun never touches. Popped it out of its roots, stripped off its clothes and jammed my teeth into it sucking. The first root of cane you've ever popped out. It feels good but it doesn't taste good. Premature but this is your effort so you eat it like it is sweet. Then you see her face pained with disgust, then her scream. Then you follow her eye and touch the mekke mekke thing with your hand and she runs. A big woman running from a snail and you run. But you can't run! How can you? You want to be a woman; now you have a man, you'll be like everybody else. You're normal now! Vomit and bear it.

Wearing my label called woman.
Upon my lapel called normal.

-You dig brother?-
-I dig-

You've got to live in an ice cage brother with your frock
turned back to front before you can be real, before you can
wear your rightful two Easter dresses and your Aunt Becca's
bag; before you can feel you have a right to walk up and
sit right down in your Granny's parlour. But this seasoning is killing me. Wish you could bust this blasted glass
for my neck is getting cricked with this looking backwards
and talking to you by tape and telephone. And cane don't
sweet in false teeth brother. Can't you salt those snails so
that I can face you, so I can chew my bounty with my own
teeth thirty-two times as I know I should . . . help . . .
please for under this nylon shroud, dry ice works my body
to a bloodless incision and my bounty into tasteless flesh . . .
I want to face you.

STILL LIFE

One

My father grew with the pale faces. He learnt from them
that a man is worthy of his hire only after he has served well
in his station; that he should stick to principles and know
his limitations: the rich man in his castle, the poor man at
his gate. That's what we learnt: of principle, the love of
the underdog and Shakespeare.

Our mother's father fought in the Boer War. The Ger-
mans called him monkey and he hated them with all his
gall but she didn't know why. The English were hypocrites
and worse than the Americans who at least told you plainly
to your face that they didn't like you. That's what he
taught her. Corpie was angry all right. He had been to
Africa and seen men's golden stools stolen and he was
angry. But Mama only knew that had he lived, she would
have known more geography.

We had patriarchs. The one pale etchings of principle,
invisible gifts of daffodils fluttering in the breeze, Ham-
letian castles and wafer disintegrating on your tongue; the
other black with anger.

I was to meet great grandfather Will again, 'the pale
one' at communion every month or so when kneeling, I
took from him the body and blood of our Lord, gobbling,
gobbling, chanting nonsense syllables registering deep in
our personal unconscious. At school he gave us Maths,
Latin and French and told us of pranks at Cambridge
where we would surely go if we did well . . . across the
sea, always across something with great-grandfather Will.
He was so nice.

But when a man don't conk you with his slate frame,
don't malice you, don't fight with you, jambing you in the

30

sides with his elbow; when you can't touch a man's anger, you can't see him, you don't know him, you don't live with him, you don't feel him. Behind the communion rails, behind the lectern, driving off with a generous smile. Great grandfather Will was romance.

You never could get Granny Tucker to admit that her grandfather had been a slave. No Sir. He was a brown man who could read and write.

You knew how to rate that. It had no name. You couldn't spell it. You could feel it : no romance there. And you didn't have trouble with figuring out Granny's touch. Slaps or a smile could travel eight miles to bring criss and ess and all manner of baked things to tease your cavities. And don't forget her words . . . threats or prayers. She was little but tallawah and she could tell any man, woman or child where to get off and the petty session was her favourite stage for Corpie had willed her anger.

But displays of anger must be trained out of the new generation. It is an Adam's apple, an indelicate bulge which appears in the throat. It must be numbed with a potage of ice. It is no play this time. It must be frozen with a compress of ice.

Two

Sam's country is beautiful. From whichever point you look, you can see green jutting into blue. On a clear day, you can feel 76 degrees fahrenheit, look up at cloudless blue skies and if you hold your head up high enough, could see snow-clad mountains. I followed him there.

They tell me you can ski on one day and drive down from the hills to swim in the sea a few hours after. It is romantic country. It is strange though. You can't sense the people because they are invisible and moreso in daylight and we were there in the season of long days . . . Just the occasional cheshire grin. I am not afraid. Sam is beautiful and firm. I can feel him. Until the day I heard their voices.

They were talking about me. Shushing at my approach but I had already heard that "Negroes in the Central Areas were ungrateful considering that our people were the first to let them fit clothes in department stores". They were shushing well talking about me and I could not answer for I could not feel them, only the big frozen lump in my throat, my ham's apple as they would call it.

But that lump is anger. Research labs now link repressed anger with cancer and the cancer must out with a surgeon's knife. No language, no public language of politeness, no communion rails now to separate the communicant and the celebrant. It is a brand new nigger war and I must find the language of abuse with which to reach them.

Every evening after five, those who look most like me, surface to take over the institution. Pushing mops, pushing pails, straightening here and there, our hard hats and chalk white teeth give me some gesture of acknowledgement: a wide smile, a half smile, even "good evening".

They are proud of me for I am a doctor and their own. Children greet me, brothers carry my parcels because I am their people. They lead me to Brown, Hughes, the lot; to funky-funk, to feel Aretha and freeze at the pig.

Strange how a common enemy tightens bonds so that we are people where once we had been men, women, carpenters, cooks, nurse's aides, doctors, light-skinned-curley-haired, black-too-dark-to-make- the TV screen. Submerged in my people, the dances of my people, the confrontations with my people, the lump in my throat dissolved, thawed into four hours of tears on my bathroom floor and I emerged from this surgery, black, taken now for an African, now for a negro, a nigger, reaching for Corpie's hand to find that I am not home.

Three

I turned around.

I faced you.

I came home to find your snail in my milk, the straw dripping slime and your lips, eyes and nose running to nothing as they did the year before.
-Is only crushed currants- You say.
Devious one, don't I know crushed snail when I see it?
Man, I have a right in this country. I have come home and I have a right to refuse to drink your snail, Mr Anancy.

Look in that spying glass as you used to as a child. You see red, you see green, you see purple flowers. Shake it and you get hibiscus, shake it again and you get roses. People say it is the crystals that form flowers. Well I am flowers too. I am home to find my place in this changing emerging mass of crystals. Yes. When I look through that penny peep hole of that view master at another school fair, I must see me in Philadelphia, USA, right here in my own back yard. When I look through another movie camera, I must see me in my Granny's front parlour, right here. That still going move man! Ah Oh.

Four

Ooooooooh. Oooooooooooh. You ever hear the men calling to one another from afar? When they throw their heads back, cup their mouths and become wood doves, their voices carry over a much greater distance. That is how they attract each other's attention and sometimes, if what they want to say is something that anybody can hear, they warble:
-Ah beg you little grass fi mi donkey oh-
-Come fah-

My father was a sawyer like his father before him and so knows all about walking in the woods and having to say "Ooooh" to track his partner down. He is going to tell me a story. He is a great story teller and I am a great story listener. He has stopped right there to let "Ooooooh" sink in and I, as he knows, am floating with his voice from the road to the bank and right up to the hillside and I already see the men. My father's voice and his face take on the features of the characters and I, wide-ackee-seed-eyed fall into a trance transmitting my spirit to each in turn, animating and incarnating them.

Today is a special day. My father is very pleased with me. I am six and little for my age yet inspector says I should be skipped to middle division, to a class of children at least five years older than I. My father is delighted. At such times, he never laughs or talks like other delighted people. He maintains silence but his eyes, a rum and water mixture, dart round the room as if he is immensely uncomfortable and the laugh lines around his mouth crease deeper from the strain of keeping his lips together. At such times he puts on a play. My father is a magician: he is a juggler and he has something up his sleeve. Now he is sitting where only children sit and has put my yam in a

35

sardine pan and is crushing and folding white yam into
white milk. Very clumsily. The fork is too small for his
hand and the tin is too small for crushing. Very unaccus-
tomed. My father is a clown. It is fascinating to watch this
adult playing just for me. He wants me to play too. That
is embarrassing : to hold masks for a big man to fool around
in. I am to be the baby to whom he feeds the white slimy
stuff. He lifts the spoon dripping slime to my mouth and I,
freezing the rest of my body, let it on to my tongue so that
he might speak :

Brer Nancy and Brer Tumbletud were partners
in the lumber business. One would stay at the
top and one would stay at the bottom of the
whipsaw, one pushing, the other pulling across
the width of the felled trees. They used to have
lunch together. And every twelve o'clock when
the school bell ring, a lady would come to the
saw pit with a basket on her head. In the basket,
she had an enamel carrier tied in a white towel.
She would help down and Brer Nancy and Brer
Tumbletud would rush to take the carrier from
her and eat.

They ate out of the same one carrier and every-
day, Nancy would tell Tumbletud :
-When I dip 'splash', you must dip 'tip'- (My
father has no face, just sounds.)

One day (and he is looking under his eyes, the
better to hit me with the punch line) hungry
Tumbletud decided that he not going to eat no
more dry food. He is going to make a splash dip.
Splash !

Brer Nancy turn pon him :
-You no hear mi sey when mi dip splash, you
fi dip tip?-

36

But Tumbletud don't even look pon him.
Splash!
Nancy get out now:
-You no hear mi sey when mi dip splash, you fi dip tip?-
Splash!
-Mi sey when mi dip splash, you fi dip tip-
Splash!
Box!
Nancy fire him one box. Him drop. Eye kin over. Him dead. Hmmm.

You ever see Tumbletud when you pass through cow pasture? Take your toe and turn him over and he will lie on his back like dead for days. Turn him over on his belly again and he will walk away just like nothing never happen. Tumbletud play that one and frightened Nancy dash through the woods as fast as his feet could carry him.

But Nancy is a man that needs company. Moreover, you can't saw without a partner. And who going to stay at the bottom of a whipsaw with you at the top if they know that you kill a man?

So Nancy decide to himself:
-Ah going to look company but ah going test them out first-
So as he walk, he say:
-Ooooooooooh-
And the echo would come back:
-Ooooooooh-
Nancy think him hear somebody warbling back.
So he throw out the rest of the message:
-You hear any news say Nancy kill Tumbletud oh-
-Nancy kill Tumbletud oh-

37

Jesus them hear, can't stay here. So Nancy rush
to the other side of the woods and try again:
-Oooooooh-
-Oooooooooh- come back.
-You hear any news say Nancy kill Tumble-
tud oh-
  -Nancy kill Tumbletud oh-
Dem hear, can't stay here.
So he try somewhere else.
-Oooooooh. Oooooooh-
-Oooooooh-
-You hear any news say Nancy kill Tumble-
tud oh-
  -Nancy kill Tumbletud oh-
  Jesus.
-Oooooooh-
-Oooooooh-
-Say Nancy kill Tumbletud oh-
-Nancy kill Tumbletud oh-

Nancy kill Tumbletud oh. Nancy spinning around in the
woods. Say Nancy kill Tumbletud oh. Oooooooh. Ooooooh.
Say Nancy kill Tumbletud oh. Me or Nancy spinning
around in the woods. Ooooooh. Ooooooh. Say Nancy kill
Tumbletud oh. Hop o my thumb, Jack on the Beanstalk
alone spinning through the woods. Say Nancy kill Tumbletud oh. I am a princess imprisoned in a cat. Nancy imprisoned in a unicorn, in a light bulb. Alone in a cabbage
leaf. Drifting from room to room, looking for my room in
the many rooms. Searching for a familiar face. In the
woods searching for my place. In the spying glass. In the
spinning mass of crystals. Nothing. Twirling madly in a
still life. Poor Nancy. Poor me.

Five

As fortune would have it, Alice joined me. Alice in Wonderland, my Aunt Alice in Wonderland slid through the sink hole and showed me the story of a man she knew:

> There was a famine in the land. It seemed like Sodom and Gommorrah. We never quite saw the land but the picture had red and brown and smokey hues suggesting that it is about to be burnt by brimstone and fire, lightning and thunder. The man rode away on a lonely donkey with no hamper under his feet and no girth under the donkey's tail. He had only determination on his face as he rode away along our dusty road which government refused to fix. He stood for the right so he was leaving, riding upright. Not swinging with the gait of the donkey as women do, nor with his feet stuck out on either side, hurrying the donkey with the seat of his body as men do. Just upright and with determination. We saw when the donkey collapsed and he walked right over the donkey's head, right up to the very end of the road where the flint stones meet the loose gravel of our roads to form the banking. Then he stopped. So close to the flint stones that he blazed and Aunt Alice showed us his etheric like halo on our coconut husk fire each ironing day and she calls it the Holy Pure Soul.

> And she showed us too the village of lean to's over cast with a four o'clock dawn. And she showed us the voice of the Holy Pure Soul ooooohing like a dog with premonitions and the villagers slowly closing their windows 'cause they don't know what he is saying.

MINIATURES

I read you Aunt Alice.

One

I came home. I listened.

-My dear chile- the woman was saying -is a good thing
you live so near. I just dying for hunger I tell you. Not
saying I criticising but you know those people live in a
different world from we. This poach egg and toast bread
and cornflakes when I must have yam and pear and bammy
for my breakfast. Even the names change my dear. Pear
don't name pear and bammy don't name bammy; is
avocado and cassava wafers. And the pee-pee chin tree
in dem front yard, it don't name so no more. Is spathodia,
if you please. Is a good thing you have me to educate
you my chile. And you can't make them know that is hard
food you want. It will shame them. So you shut your
mouth. Is the least a mother can do. But I glad you living
so near. Fancy I can sit at your door way and lap mi frock
between mi knee and drink this peasoup and cut my
dumpling with the spoon. Up there, we don't drink soup.
Is broth we get and everybody have to finish it before the
real food come. Then you should see it when it come. Like
the lady say is "Lil scraps a dis, lil scraps a dat, lil scraps
a warawara". But is what I send him to school for. And
is the least a mother can do. Can't let down the side now.
But I glad you live down the lane where I can lap mi
frock between mi knee and drink this banana water.-

Two

I came home to see. . . .

The french windows were wide open and curtainless. The floor scrubbed clean waiting for its shine. The tables, chairs, settee all seemed scrubbed and waiting too for something . . . a cushion, a mat, some varnish . . ? In the kitchen the man and the woman stood despite the chairs, staring past each other. Waiting. Perhaps for a language. And in the common room, the men sat at the bar. Tall men, handsome men, learned men, black men, sat on their stools, twirling their glasses, twirling their seats in unison and always to the right, staring in the direction of the road. Wordlessly in unison, waiting. Waiting for what? Perhaps for their women. But aren't they all around them! Some even at home? Then what are they waiting for?

Three

I came home.

-You can't swim and you from the islands?-
-No I can't swim and neither can my brothers and we live near the sea-
-Could your father swim?-
-Of course-
-Then how come?-
-You don't understand. We would have drowned-
-I've seen your Blue Hole. It really is one of the wonders of the world. Perched on top of that very high mountain out there in the wilderness! You can hardly believe it-
-I believe you-
-The smell of it. The moss. Where would one get moss of that kind in the hills. The sea must have been there once. Heavens! you can see the creation unfolding before your very eyes. And the city at sundown. I hand it to you. You have a lovely place-
-You've lost me there-
-Eh?-
-Nobody has spoken of it like that before-
-Eh?-
-I haven't heard anyone talk in such terms before.-
-You mean you haven't seen it?-
-Never-
-But how? It is only seven miles from the City.-
-You don't understand what it is like to be a parent in this country-
-I must also believe that you haven't enjoyed what the brochures say you all enjoy. That you don't know how nice it is to sit under the coconut tree and break open your own coconuts?-
-You are perfectly right-

42

-But your father can-

-And my uncles too. They know how to use the machete-

-You did say you were brought up on a farm?-

-Yes-

-Then how?-

-We might have harmed ourselves-

-Oh yes. I don't understand what it is like to be a parent in this country. I suppose you have no rhythm either?-

-True but you have seen my Auntie. The stories are true. We do have rhythm but that was of yesteryear. Now we have learning. We were brought up to take to learning. To take to Plato and Moses.-

-The cave and all that. Oh yes, you've seen the light-

-Yes I have seen the light and I shall lead my people-

-Lead?-

Four

I came home.

Name : Ida Jenkins.
Age : 34.
Address : 125, Spanish Town Road.

Miss Jenkins was referred to our agency for assistance in getting her twelve year old daughter, Gertrude, to join its putative father Adolphus Henry overseas. Mr Henry has never supported the child nor accepted paternity before but he has recently married a woman who has had a hysterectomy and has no children of her own. Gertrude and her putative father have never met and Miss Jenkins, we suspect, has not been in touch with Mr Henry since he left the island ten years ago. Gertrude is Miss Jenkins' only child. A discussion with Miss Jenkins to make sure that she appreciates all the implications of this move is indicated.

-How are you?-

-OK-

-So you want to send Gertrude to join her father- I smiled invitingly.

-Yes- She doesn't smile, fawn, want anything from me. I try again with my inviting, social working smile :

-Tell me about it-

-Nothing to tell really. Opportunities much better there and his wife can't have any children-

-But you only have one or am I wrong?-

-Only Gertie-

-I suppose you could have more if you wanted-

-Yes, but I won't be having any more- This woman strange, Lord.

-Oh you've been taking the birth control !-

-No- This woman mad, Lord.
-But you sound so sure. You have a good many child-bearing years ahead of you, you know-
She broke into an educative and, yes, superior smile :
-I have accepted the Lord as my personal saviour-

Yes, Lord that's faith. Peter stand on the seas. Works without faith is not enough, not enough, the Father has said. So where is my faith? So who must lead whom? Who must teach whom? No Sir, swimming cannot be taught. So where please is my faith, my God, my man?

Five

My young man's got the spirit. He's turned over a new leaf. He's even changed his profession. He is going to get more learning so that he can better minister to his people. My young man loves his people. He gives half of his salary to his people. My young man talks in an unknown tongue . . . words like 'underdevelopment', 'Marx', 'cultural pluralism'. I love my young man. He's got the black spirit and it's riding him hard. Lead on Robin. Lead on.

TO WALTZ WITH YOU

One

25, 5th street houses a government yard. The term government yard denotes a set of ten rectangular rooms joined together. Each room is of the same exact size as the other and has the same exact fittings. Directly behind these rooms is a set of ten smaller rooms, rectangular too but smaller than the above. These rooms too are joined laterally and carry the same exact fittings in each: a water closet marked 5th street, reg. no. 35, a toilet, a shower, and a tiny wash basin.

A little further away is a large cooking area. Why this section is not divided into ten cubicles, to complete the pattern, is the architect's private secret.

25, 5th street has a gate with a tiny porter's lodge. Apart from 25, 5th street, there are 19, 21 and as many yards as there are odd numbers up to 35. There is no point in describing them. They are all like 25, 5th street. This is where we live and have our being. In all the odd numbers.

Sitting in the lodge is a brown woman. She is very hard. Everything about her says 'hard'. She is fattish, seally fat and you can see that under her dress, she wears a long line bra and girdle. You know that if you touch her, the compressed fat-beneath-the bone would fail to give. She is hard. She never leaves her seat but you can, every second, hear the 'clang clang' as her crochet needle hits against her thumb-nails. Intricate patterns she must be crocheting because it never ends. Hard up-standing woman. The doctors say she doesn't pee . . . stones in her bladder.

Government houses are built as the name suggests by the government for the people . . . for us the indigent, who have been made so by fire, hurricane or some other catastrophe. The house is a gift but on our shoulders lie the cost of its maintenance. To keep the roofs from springing leaks, the toilets and sinks in working condition, we the occupiers pay 25 cents every time we leave the premises. This is our responsibility; this is our contribution to our welfare.

Truth to tell, we hardly leave for we have no skills to offer and no funds to pay our exit fee. Miss D in the porter's lodge does the collecting. She is supposed to be Mr D's assistant but no one has ever seen Mr D. We suspect that she is also Mr D. She is as old as the scheme and has never been known to let through 24 cents. Miss D is hard. Beg her a chance, a cent just dropped through your fingers into the drain and she says "Wait 'til the cleaner man comes to clean it out, then bring me the right amount. I can't do that kind of thing. You want me to get in trouble nuh. You want Mr D to come kill me." The D's, in any case Miss D, must know how hard it is for us to find 25 cents. We came into the scheme with nothing . . . destitute. She has been at the lodge half-sharing our existence for centuries now. There is no way she could not know that.

Yes, it is a hard life however you look at it but we, at least, are trying. Egbert keeps our hearts warm with the promise of the second coming. Errol always finds time to tell us what is in those big volumes he is always reading and we hear about the millenium dawn when we shall truly rule ourselves. Barry doesn't read; he thinks it is bull shit. Pardon me but Barry is like that. But he thinks. He thinks we'll get a cross between the two — a second coming but a theocracy and then we'll be angels, black angels. Beatrice is rough: but never you mind; her bark is worse than her bite. She can always find time and cloth to make a bandage or two and to put a patch here and there and she is good with a darning needle and don't our small clothes need it!

I do my small part. I take the minutes of the regular weekly meetings.

There are some of us who don't try at all. No need to

hide it. We have unfortunately to make a distinction between them and us. Those people throw dice, slam dominoes and give-laugh-for-peasoup all day long. They have no culture, no sense of identity, no shame or respect for themselves. Those people would climb through the barbed-wire fence, mingle shamelessly with the people beyond, beg them rum and cigarettes and creep back into the compound. They have no culture at all. No interest in helping their leaders keep their heads up high. We get no co-operation from them. How will we ever lead them out in the right and proper way, through the front gate, past the turnstile, past Miss D, proud, skilled, cultured and tall? Bad as she be Miss D knows who is who though. She never questions us when we ask for extra toilet paper and she makes every effort, over and beyond her call of duty to give us the books and writing paper that we need. She knows leadership when she sees it.

Two

The night my young man got caught up in the spirit and burnt to grease like beef suet caught in a dutchie pot, I wept so hard, my tears no longer held salt. Such a frightfully humiliating way to die! But I went on as before. I took the minutes with a stiff upper lip. Egbert read the lesson. He reminded us of the transfiguration, of how Elijah and Christ became one (I had not seen that meaning before) and how it was quite unnecessary for one to build tabernacles when such a spiritual fusion had taken place. I knew he meant well. I know that he was saying that my young man had burnt to ash, that he wouldn't even get a headstone nor six foot six of earth but none of that was important since his spirit lived in us. But I was not a spirit. Or at any rate not only spirit. And I couldn't help but know that Robin had once had body too. We had been bodies : and what was there to show for it?

Errol tried too to comfort me. He tried to pretend that nothing had happened. Errol explained once more in detail the significance of the prefix *demos*. I would have thought that by now he would have exhausted every angle but I watched in fascination as he moved us from *Demosthenes* to *demagogue,* as he split it into *de/mo*s to make the 'most for them', as he showed how 'm' contracted into 'n' in accordance with the earliest usage of the language, made *demos* mean among us. All of which was to prove for the nth time that from any angle you looked at it, "the people were destined to come into their own". I know he meant this speech to mean that my young man had not died in vain.

Today, in deference to me, Barry used no swear words and shifted his thesis from the significance of the term 'sally water' in folk children's ring games to the examination of the significance of the term 'imgaan'. He was not

52

subtle, but then Barry never had been. He has a good heart. But a good heart cannot heal my pain unless it makes some connection with mine. In their kindliness, they were trying to keep me from breaking down. But I wished to God that they would give me a chance to cry it out with all of me. But who would dig a trench to flow my tears to them. No. I had to sweat them out. That was our way. Suddenly, it struck me that our path lead to dessication. We were bent on exterminating water : there could never be a trench of tears between us; that Robin had reached our highest phase of evolution : he had become a dried up bird and could only crumble into dust. I saw that it was us who had killed Cock Robin.

It struck me that everyone else knew this, even Beatrice. It struck me that the minutes I kept truly ticked us into urns. Such a line of thinking I knew was foolish but I was suddenly strongly aware that I wanted a grave beneath the earth with flowers and the sound of raucous Baptist singing; that such thoughts made me a loner; that such thoughts made me subversive; that such thoughts made me even more powerless than the rest of us; that I had best give up such thoughts at least for the time being.

That night I broke one of the informal rules or perhaps I should use the passive : one of the informal rules was broken by me. I wandered purely by chance into the gambling den. No-one recognised me and I knew no one. This is not surprising. There is very little mixing between them and us. This act of mine shamed me and I wept copiously. Not because I had stepped out of caste or anything like that but because this act was a subconscious/unconscious one and I feared that this meant that I was losing my grip on myself. As does not surprise you, I'm sure, this awareness made me lose my grip even further. As I worried about it, I wept and wept because I shouldn't weep ... and so on. I just wept.

-No mi dear, you can't walk 'round crying like that- somebody said.

It was a new experience to have people hugging me and drying my tears. And somebody else said:

-What happen. Is you guy beat you up. Don't shame- And I wished I could have said yes. Things would have made so much more sense. So I wept. I wept for the things I hadn't felt, I wept for the things I had felt. I wept for all experiences whether I had experienced them or not. I wept for all people and all things they could possibly weep for. I wept till I had obscured all reason for weeping. I just wept. And someone reprimanded:

-Blasted idiot, dry your eyes- and kissed the brush of my afro. That had never happened before. I couldn't see his face for he kissed me from behind and vanished into the crowd but I will always remember his smell — a smell of sweet lime — a scent I recognised from the days outside. Surely he had recently been outside! He had to be one of those who couldn't wait, who stole out of the compound by illegal means. One of those against whom my spirit ought to feel especially revolted.

But that kiss, despite the donor, made it possible for me to carry on.

Three

It was the first of August that I met him again. I remember it clearly for it was on the day of our think-in — Emancipation Day. We have always had a marathon 'think-in' to mark Emancipation Day. Errol came with someone. He always felt that that was good : it pointed out to the masses that we relied on them and were happy to co-operate with them. Errol more than any of us meant this and did all in his power to let them feel welcome if they wandered in or if they showed the slightest interest in rapping with us. He felt it was key to let them know that they too were the architects of our freedom.

I smelt the sweet lime and knew at once but I didn't want to face him. I didn't want to see him. Not yet.

He said nothing in the first meeting. It didn't matter. I wasn't embarrassed. One has to learn and after all if he had missed the track as he obviously had done, it could take a considerable amount of exposure to follow the gist of what we were saying (Not me really. The fellows. I was taking down notes for all I was worth). The fellows discussed matters slowly. Repeated some of the basic premises with which we were all familiar after years of being together. All this for what we hoped would be a new recruit. It was boring for me much less for them ! Imagine going over first year notes and pretending to treat them seriously ! There were even confrontations which we knew were mock confrontations for we had gone through them years before and had learnt what there was to learn from them. But only by sinking to the level of the new recruit can you hope to proselytise him. Our new recruit said nothing. Not even to ask questions for clarification. To top it all, he left before the end. I thought that was very unfortunate for after all, even he must see that we were bending backwards to accommodate him. I felt sorry for

Errol when he left; we were left high and dry and it was his guest that caused it. How do you return a graduate type seminar to its former level after you have pitched your discussion at Sunday School level. The calamity, happily brought us closer and we pitched in with renewed vigour to discuss the relative contributions of the Saints and the Merchants to the promulgation of the Emancipation Act. Barry moved for the adjournment with the none-too-subtle offering, "Rome was not built in a day".

Next Wednesday, our new recruit was back bright and early. Barry welcomed him with one of his obscenities. I don't approve of such language but I felt that coming from where he was coming that kind of welcome was likely to make him feel at home. So I smiled. Generally into space. I did not want to catch his eye or show any sign of friend-liness because I felt that he should get a fair chance to know everybody else, to know what we were really about, because, let's face it, people sometimes come into an organ-isation for strange sorts of reasons. We are all familiar with the stories of men who pretend to be 'saved' just so they could have carnal knowledge of some woman. There was no reason to believe that this fellow would suddenly drop the ways of outside!

This time, he stayed to the end and still asked no ques-tions. This time Errol explained all the procedures to him. This time the fellows talked directly to him rather than around him and stopped at every point to make sure that he understood. At the end of the session, Egbert expressed the hope, on behalf of all of us, that he felt like one of us and that he would return. In reply, he said that he had found the session quite *stimulating* and *exciting*. He could not have used those words if he had not been able to follow us all along! The funny thing, though, was that he address-ed his words in my direction. There was something not quite straight about the man.

56

He was to come back to every meeting we had for six weeks and he asked not a question and made no points. This was indeed our gimme-mi-bit egg! I felt that he could do better than that. I felt too that there was some deliberate plan that he was waiting for us to recognise. Even patient Egbert was getting annoyed. Things began to break. On this day in particular, I read the regular weekly minutes as usual and Egbert called for their confirmation. There was silence. By some informal sanction, the mover of the motion for confirmation changes from week to week so that every member of the body gets a chance at it. He must have sensed this for he had been to our meetings regularly enough and long enough and he was no fool. He could not help knowing that we were waiting on him. Egbert glanced at him and I could measure in that glance the effort to keep calm. I glanced at him and I saw the smirk. We waited. He did not do the decent thing. Errol felt forced to retrieve the situation and to confirm the minutes. The meeting dragged on for a time. Naturally . . . it would, until we could find some way of disposing of the incident. We could not simply forget him or it for that would be contrary to our philosophy. That way was closed to us. It was our burden to treat with the incident and learn what we could from it. Any action of censure against him even at the psychological level would have to be initiated and carried out by him. That was our way. People assumed responsibilities for themselves. If a problem necessitated the removal of an individual that individual was expected to undertake such removal of himself. The ball was clearly in his court. We rightly expected some corrective response from him.

And do you know that at the end of the meeting he did not have the grace to vanish as was obviously called for! He stood around small-talking and smiling with that smile at everyone as if he was the master of the occasion. I could not avoid it this time. I had to look at the man. The nerve of the man! And he stared dry-eyed at me before the whole host of fellows, making a silent statement of war right there. I was angry. After all what right had he to undermine our meeting in that way? If he had doubts why not keep them to himself? We all had doubts, I'm sure but we submerged them for the good of the whole. He knew our philosophy would not allow us to throw him out as he deserved or even to snub him so he was really hitting us the dirtiest of blows as he well knew. He even knew Barry's obscenities for show and that there was no way that Barry could curse him out as he would like us to feel he could.

Accursed limed smelling man! Hit me with a feather if beneath all that beard, that neatly plaited hair, the new bright crinkled corners of the eye, the haughtiness, the unabashed stare, the paler, more polished complexion, the man of the world air, the colgate toothpaste well kept teeth, it was not Baba whom I had last seen at school close on twenty years ago!

Four

In that moment of recognition, three things flashed across my mind : (a) I had sensed that night, that the man who held me by the shoulders to kiss my hair had not been holding me for the first time. (b) A two minute scene came back. I was nine, I remembered. He must have been ten or eleven. We were going on an outing to Town and passing the Spanish Town lock-up. I heard again Baba saying from the top of the truck, "Look, is there so". I remembered that the rest of us, the whole truck, it seemed, looked, touched those who had not seen it and said, "Look is there so". I remember being puzzled then and even as a big woman passing by that place, I would feel puzzled. No one had bothered to ask "Is there so what"? I could see now, that coming from the country bush like the rest of us, Baba was no better placed than the rest of us to point out landmarks. It struck me too that we must have somewhere realised this but for some reason preferred to mask the question and to accept his definitions. And there were other like incidents in our pre-teens which were only beginning to surface now . . . how Baba could rob me of a chance to tell Mass Stanley's stories and yet not tell them himself . . . a bubble-burster,a wet blanket, one-who-would-not-let-you-dream, a know-it-all. His thoughts were facts : he knew where he was going; he was right. He did not need to discuss it or even to tell anyone what made him right. And people accepted this. They just let him lead. He didn't need you. You couldn't make suggestion. You resented it, but you were afraid to leave. His doctor's kit. The chocolate tree was the hospital whether you agreed or not. And you let him lead though the mulatto companion tree was much shadier and had far more gadgets. The chocolate tree it had to be. He never moved.

(c) I relived too in my mind a film in which a handsome Haitian man pursued a couple relentlessly with no more weapons than a smile and a doll. I saw once more that couple plunge from a precipice while that man and his smile remained constant. The power of the self-assured. My mind had made four with this man before. Baba had mellowed into that frighteningly self-assured man. He had made himself into that Haitian obeah man. Still, I was more angry than frightened. Baba could have accosted me openly or at least more openly. And even so, why accost? And why the fellows? He was quite aware of what he was doing to them. He was aware that he held all the cards and whatever his point, there were more straight-forward ways of fighting, for a fight, it surely was now.

Baba, Harris Ruddock as he now was (had always been in truth, though we had never thought to call him that), was never absent, never late for any of our next four meetings. He had affected whittling now. It was pear seeds. In the first meeting for the month, he carved a head. While we struggled to make and match intellectual points under the weight of a hostile stranger, as if snatching and using our strength, he'd press his knife into the pear seed and whittle out the side of the nose and so on until the whole face was done. Narrowing his eyes, furrowing his lips, he worked hard throughout the meeting and seemed to have timed the end of the face to match its end. He'd leave with the sculpture in his pocket but not without his usual chit-chat, the manner of which never changed. Clearly he had not changed towards us, it was we who had changed!

In our next meeting, he made the neck and the arms. It was a child. We knew. We were watching, obviously seduced from the fight to rescue him for our philosophy. As usual he left with his art in his pocket but only after the statutory chit-chat. The third meeting saw the hip. In the fourth meeting we got the legs and knew that the image was sexless.

Baba was absent from the fifth and sixth meetings but that brought us no relief. We all knew that we were waiting for him to come, that he called our tune, that we were squibs whose strings he had pulled and that we could now only make a puff. He arrived at our seventh meeting as if nothing had happened. Egbert tried to behave as if he were an ordinary member. He welcomed him, remarked his absence and hoped that nothing had been amiss with him. No he had been quite all right, just bogged down with work. He did not disappoint us. He drew from his pocket the baby all held together by a stick run vertically through its body and began to burnish it.

This time when Egbert called for the minutes to be confirmed, he stuck up his hand as we used to do at school when we sought permission to talk or to be let out, came across to me where I had the minute book on my lap and put the baby on it. Pear seed when dry becomes very brittle. If you put a stick through its middle, it is bound to crumple to pieces. The baby crumbled in my lap into sixteen pieces, four for each day, four for each pear seed. In those two weeks of absence, he must have been parching the doll. Baba had made his point and he left.

How unnecessary, how unoriginal and rude!

My minutes as I knew and needed no one to tell me, had run me into a cracked up doll. The message was there for all of us to interpret. We had seen it coming. We had each secretly guessed what he intended to do. It could be applied to us singly or as a group. Baba's point was that we should stop hiding and talk about ourselves. Quite reasonable. I had thought it myself in my private sorrow and been afraid. But I was mad. I was livid. I was damned angry on every front and you can see why. He had crumbled us just as effectively as he had crumbled that doll. We had seen it coming and we had been powerless to act, to let him know that he was a boor who did not understand the rules of our game. Who made him God? Who told him that he could touch parts of us that we elected to leave untouched! A challenge had been given to me and a challenge I would take. I would beard that low-down, high-handed outsider in his den and let him have all he'd been asking for.

So help me God I would do it.

Five

Baba was waiting for me. Straight and tall in a long white
gown. He was the bride. His hair neatly plaited (as usual)
and his beard obviously brushed. His finger nails which
had never been like ours, were even more remarkable
now . . . half moons neatly outlined, no hang-nail and just
enough of a white oval excess pointing each finger tip, to
balance the half-moons. You guessed it! He was wearing
Jesus sandals with straps twisted at the ankles and obviously going further up his leg to where I could not see.
The man exuded the clean astringent atmosphere of lime.
It was as if he had been cured, scrubbed, cleansed in lime.
What a beauty! His hands, as I knew from memory were
soft as a surgeon's hands but without the puttiness. As he
held them shepherd-like out to me, I could see that even
the criss-crosses which most of us blacks have indelibly in
our palms were missing from his. Perhaps he had been
soaked in lime while the rest of us passed through a seasoning of ice! I had not heard that he had gone to foreign
lands to study and I could not think for the life of me, of
any land which grew limes but our own. His seasoning
must have been done . . .

-Right here- he said smiling his relaxed, at home, pastoral
smile. I saw red. Even if he could read the furrows of my
brows and guess at my question, he had no right to give it
voice. Couldn't this man understand that people had a right
to privacy?

I brushed past his extended arms and flounced into a
white wooden slat chair. It was necessary to sustain my
mood of anger and aggression and although I have an
innate curiosity about the inside of people's houses, I
didn't want to look around lest any of my charge should
dissipate. I couldn't help noticing though, how sanctified
his little room looked. The floor was of plain concrete,

63

the shiny kind on which jacks balls and marbles bounce high. He had two single vono-beds touching in an L-shape, each with its sheet tucked under its mattress so you could see clear under the beds. Light and air filtered in above them and would forever do so through the slat windows which I knew had been transformed so that they could be thrown wide open in the hotter summer days. (Now why hadn't we thought of that?) This abode wished to hide nothing. On the far side to my right beginning from the roof and ending mid-way down the wall were shelves of well-kept hard cover books. The shelf arrangement gave the lid of the desk below, just enough room to avoid collision if ever it was opened. There was one straight-backed chair at the desk. I was sitting at the one easy chair, slatted as if to match the windows. Under my feet was a square straw mat which integrated bed (sleeping area), desk (study area) and entertaining area (the chair on which I sat) in a clean, immaculate, translucent unity. You could see under everything.

I was wondering where the passage that broke the line of the wall beside him led and how come he had an extra apartment and whether it was as sanctified as this, when he broke into my thoughts :

-I cut a wall through to the kitchen and yes. It is as sanctified as this. There is no point to clutter. Take the essence out and throw away the chaff. Somebody else might need it-

These last two sentences he addressed directly into my eyes. A neat put down. Could I now talk about how he had mashed up our play thing? I was burning even brighter with anger. But what was I to say? I would relax and let his talk infuriate me into action.

-That bed across from you is yours. I know you like fresh air.- His face was quite serious and matter-of-fact. There was nothing for me to do but flounce out.

Six

After all that cleanliness, I did not see how to go back to my stifling little room with all the loose leaves and stencilled pamphlets in red, green, yellow (in any colour you want just name it), our work, Robin's and mine. I hadn't had the heart to clean up after his burning and to be honest, there was no motivation. We just didn't bother with that kind of thing. The fact that bits of his fat had congealed on most of the papers and had stuck them willy-nilly into groups of uneven sizes and shapes, made the cleaning up task virtually impossible for all kinds of reasons which you can well imagine. Grease, dust and ash are an unbeatable team. I felt a traitor as I was walking round avoiding my room, comparing ours with his, for that was really comparing Baba with Robin and the rest of us and I knew that if I pursued that line . . . I would not pursue that line. Besides, my skin was feeling very dry and prickly : the kind of thing that happens when there is a fever in your blood. The moving liquid stops just a while to tickle you here and before you can really scratch, it rushes elsewhere to tickle you again. There was and is really no point in scratching : the thing just runs too fast. My best bet was to keep in perpetual motion so the blood's rate of flow would be forced to keep pace with mine and have no time to tickle my dermis.

-Poor chile. She studying too much. Is the man you know. Just burn up so. Is the reaction. A late reaction you know. It just set in now. Some people don't feel it same time you know. It take long before it hit them. Soon gone off her head. Poor thing . . .-

I had not realised that I was making a public spectacle of myself. That my movements were attracting attention. I was the object of pity. My little scheme for personal discipline was pointless; might as well scratch too. Moreover, if my

65

finger nails tore my skin as sometimes happens on these occasions, that would no doubt help to dissolve the lump now beginning to gather in my throat. So I scratched and walked. Walking fast and scratching, I know I looked like a fowl in an ants' nest but I didn't mind; there were secondary gains in playing to the gallery. I think I had a right to their pity. After all, how many women's men burn to ash? I had a perfectly good claim to being a martyr if they so felt like treating me.

I did not and do not feel however that I had any claims to being an angel so I cannot explain the levitation. As I walked and scratched in my circle, my body lifted itself into the air and I became nothing. Light. Without even a dream in my mind. If weighed in the balance, my dear Aunt, I would no doubt be found wanting.

They tell me that the doctors tried their best but that since I wasn't wearing my diabetic medal, it was sometime before they could prescribe. A little sugar, they say, brought me back. Just as well I had blacked out. I couldn't have helped them. That I was a diabetic was news to me. No one in my family was and we had no history of fainting. Asthma was more our line. I wondered . . . I couldn't help it.

Miss Gibson was fat and fair and new to school. New to the area and new to teaching. She smelt nice and she looked nice and she made everybody smile. She had us all in the palm of her hands without even trying. Teacher Norton especially. He couldn't even cane when she was around. After five years of resisting assistant teachers who had come and gone, who had stayed on to try harder, when the field had narrowed to Miss Rose and Miss Pinks, Miss Gibson walked in and within three months and with the approval of the whole community, parents and children alike, had managed to get Teacher Norton to buy her what we had never ever met before, an engagement ring.

66

Then her fainting spells started and even us in the lower division, knew that Miss Gibson had been inflicted.

The practice of medicine is a strange thing and we can't always accept their diagnosis. I had seen this thing before hadn't I? Those circles I was walking, were they natural, or had I been forced to walk them? Was there a power trying to get me back to this room? To this bed? I knew Baba's past. He knew mine. On this we shared a common language. And hadn't I seen him recently at work! And how did one explain his difference from us? His calm, his peace, his ease. The man was dabbling in a higher science but I was just too tired to think about it.

Amid the smell of beef soup and ginger tea, the commotion of tipping toes and tired thoughts, I recognised the feel of Baba's index finger tracing the sweat around the baby hairs of my forehead, saw his smile and heard his:

-Welcome back you lucky creature. You too know what the resurrection is like. You have a clean slate, you can start all over again-

It had a warmth and a human-ness that was a far cry from an 'infliction'.

Seven

I did get my beef soup, my egg nog and my regular shots of insulin but away from the hurly-burly of philosophical theses, my emotions began to take over from my mind and great gushes of tears, it seemed, wanted to be let out of my head. It needed acupuncture. It needed a human basin that could hold my tears-letting. He could do it. I had experienced the firm gentleness of his probing fingers. With just his index finger he had probed the base of my skull that day, had made me sweat and broken my fever. He could draw water from the brain. Did I not know that?

He was not like Egbert and Barry and the other fellows. He still had oodles of moisture. I could hear the water in his voice when he welcomed me back and even now could see the perspiration making patterns on the back of his thin white shift. His tears could absorb mine! I had met his bottomless pool. He knew about tears. And had I not good reason to cry? How many women have seen their men reduced to a little bit of smoke, just enough to hold in an inkwell! Together we could make a flood that would give me a cleaner slate on which to start again. But he wouldn't let me cry. He wouldn't touch me.

No sooner would I wax into the tear jerking story of our lives, of whose fault it was that we had been kept apart, of what might have happened if we hadn't been kept apart, than he would say:

-I have heard it all before.-

I developed master strategies for creeping it in, for dragging it in, sneaking it in backways, sideways:

-Poor Robin. He never did have a chance. And I couldn't help him. I should have met you earlier . . . - but he would say:

-I see it coming. At this point I withdraw- And like a snail, he would curl up into himself. A little bit of sweat

68

but no tears and a snail's sweat can hardly even erase a common 'i' much less erase a whole slate's markings. Once he even left physically but his withdrawals were matter-of-factly, emotionally controlled and never in anger. At his most disgusted he would say :

-I only want to meet you-

But wasn't that what I was working for? That his tears should meet mine. Weren't we in essence water. Wasn't that why we couldn't fly? I was essentially water and so was he. We were real and if we were to meet, then what more honest way than through our tears! He had told me time and time again that our solutions lay in our liquidity. He had spent a good long time in teaching me that, in pointing out to me that I was more than a cracked up doll. I had seen for myself that levitation was not for me. I had fainted. I was water. I belonged to the earth. I was not like Aunt Becca had said, 'wanting'. I had been weighed in the balance and finally found heavy enough to sink. There was a purpose to me and it lay through water, through his tears and mine. Wasn't that the lesson? Or was this obeah man of an anancy trying to play something else on me!

I even stripped one night and though he was obviously excited, he said just as matter-of-factly as at any other time :

-That will come later. After I have met you.-

Blast him.

He reduced me to hysterical screams.

-I don't know the machinations of those people's lives.- He had me screaming and I don't scream.

-You don't?- he asked as if we were having a rational argument, as if he had never parried in an emotional field.

It was now nearly six weeks since my illness and I had

69

recovered considerably. I wanted to try my legs. True the room was extremely comfortable and I had the best nurse but I wanted to feel my strength, to test my becoming. For the longest while I had been asking Baba to take me out . . . anywhere. I needed to know myself in my world. It was not a pool of water, a placenta. If it had been, he would have cried with me into peace, calm and security. And it certainly could not be the immaculate egg of a room in which we lived. I was being choked again. I needed out. For some inexplicable reason which everybody seemed to accept and to understand, I couldn't go back to the meeting house and the brothers stopped visiting me. We all agreed, it seemed, that there was a parting of the ways. My path lay now through the aliens who surrounded me. It is one thing to wander into their quarters, to put on a show for them and quite another to live from day to day with them. I was willing to learn their ways but someone had to show me, to born me. Someone had to help me make my debut. Someone had to help me test my feet outside the kumbla.

Tonight there was going to be a dance.

-The music sounds good- I had said, jigging to convince him.

-It sounds good- he said -but I won't be there-

-But I want to go (After all I had been through, I needed some consideration !)-

-Well. Why don't you go?- he had said with that pained expression on his face that suggested that he couldn't imagine what could stop me from going. The fraud.

-Can't you see that I am a woman. (Wrong question. He probably hadn't)-

-I can see that you are a woman and a very fine specimen at that. But what has that got to do with the dance-

-I'll go alone- I had muttered more to end a recurring

70

argument that never more than skimmed the surface of my mood, than to excite conversation. But he didn't stop.

-That's just it- he sparkled -A woman alone and attractive. You won't miss a dance-

It was here that I screamed registering even in the heights of my emotion only the tiniest bit of my frustration with the word plays, word plays, word plays, the resistance to communication. Words are so inadequate! -Sweetheart- he tenderly, so tenderly said, -I know you want to give yourself but I fear that you offer yourself because you don't want you. That's no gift love, even if we did need gifts. That's something you throw on a scrap-heap. We won't forage for a thing in a scrap-heap. We need a walk-ing-talking human being-

You understand this petti-fogging man who is to look at me and tell me after all these weeks of building up, of taking me from a life I knew, who is to look at me now and tell me that I have no worth. You understand this damned shameless rasta-man who is to tell me that he wants to watch me grow. You understand this r . . .-c . . . t of a hungry man from nowhere who is to watch and observe me. What the hell he think he is. Man don't let me . . . I had been talking aloud. Is that me? with such expressions. Am I a fishwife?

-Yes it is you. You have found your language, Ma'am- he said with a new kind of calm. I thought unhappily that I had really touched a soft spot with my reference to the obscurity of his past. But his smile was as tender as before.

-Next thing you'll be telling me where I come from and that would really be telling as you know-

And with even more tenderness, he sat me in our easy chair and kneeling before me, traced my hairline with his index finger.

-You must be exhausted- he said, with that tender half

71

smile that could make me feel like a princess. I luxuriated in my new found royalty.

-Your dermis is beginning to show and it is beautiful-
Me the awakened sleeping beauty, he Prince Charming.

I relaxed deep down in the slats of the chair about to cup this love, when he asked in his master's voice:

-Aren't you supposed to be going somewhere-

Eight

You must be right, Aunt Becca, you must be right. Those people so different — different from us.

In my six weeks of convalescence, I could hear their shuffling in the kitchen and assumed they were fat women. Heard the jingle of the toilet chain and heard the rush of the water. Heard the slam of the dominoes and could imagine the men with cigarettes illicitly and precariously popped at the side of their mouths, squinting their eyes from deep concentration and the smart of the cigarette smoke. Could imagine them putting aside a key card and arranging the other six in their two palms with the thumbs curled over to protect their 'play' from gaze though no-one ever tried to peep. These people were to me neutral patterns of sounds and smells, visual memories from my long past.

The little hall throbbed like a racing pulse. All those sounds and smells were compressed into a living animal called the 'hall'. I might have shrunk back; nobody could have noticed me. There was no body. The hall was too strong and potent an animal and too far removed from me to notice me. Baba would not have closed his door on me had I returned but I have always been acutely aware that any man who putting his hand to the plough looks back, becomes a pillar of salt, needs to be thawed all over again, to go through the same experiences all over again and will have to meet the people under the same circumstances, no better equipped, at another time.

If I could concentrate on a piece of the hall, I could reduce it, I was sure, to manageable proportions. I was sure that though it represented itself as a perfect round, there was some opening, some seam somewhere. I pushed aside all music, all smells and concentrated on the formal structure. The windows began to appear and as my eyes

73

became accustomed to the lighting, I realised that a part of the round, represented the hunched shoulders of men sitting on what must be a verandah rail, rounding their shoulders, to keep their balance or to protect the beer bottles between their legs. As my eyes traversed the round of their backs, I could make out a wooden arch. My past experiences told me that this must be the entrance and that here there must be the gateman. I was right about the first but there was no gateman. There was no formal rite of passage.

Nine

-Why didn't they tell me that the coffee has white blossoms that smell of Tia Maria? Or that Madam Faith ties the whole bank side with white in June?- Baba shrugged his shoulders but I couldn't stop.

-Or that the kiss-me-quick has huge nut brown thorns and delicate red velvet petals or even that the growing cane smells sweet like sugar?-

-You are learning- is all he said, with that educated smile that I had come to like.

> Last night I let myself into a new world. I simply walked in. Nobody pressed me back, nobody asked my fare, nobody asked my name, nobody saw me, nobody noticed me. I stepped on toes, was squashed by rumps in mento, had my face scratched by flailing hands, but by now had learnt to say 'Ouch' and pass on as happened when I ground toes. The light was no brighter but this piece of ground was clearly mine no more or less than anybody else's; I had a right to sense my way in and around bodies and spirits. The amalgam is a thrashing moving thing: the music of laughter, sighs, ouches, of the saxophone, of tramping shifting feet keeps the tempo going, round and up like the steam in a boiling house so that even the round stick rafters are us.
>
> Some people analyse that spirit and perceive each individual atom. Alice could: for how else would she have been able to recognise me and call me by my name?
>
> I travelled with her, my Aunt Alice, my father's mother's sister Alice Whiting who never could settle down to housewifing but spent her

earthly days visiting with and washing for the fading ones. I travelled with her inside that round and she showed me our gardens. I saw the shine deep green of the coffee trees and smelt their white flowers. She told me of Tia Maria. I saw the cocky fingers of Madam Faith; she told me about her powers. She made me taste the guinea hen weed and the leaf of life, for better vision, she said. Things began to take shape. I could see the round sticks and the four A's of the roof of the boiling house. Truly, there's neither exit nor entrance. Just eight stout round sticks which hold up the roof, with four or five slimmer sticks fitting into every two uprights for us to sit or lean or what have you. I saw a dais in the middle where the copper would have been and saw what must be musicians forming a sort of centre piece which I knew from playing with a spying glass, would change in colour and in shape but never change its locus. I saw too the myriad pieces of crystal littered round this base — those bits of glass which change their colours, shapes and positions to form now green, now yellow petals in the kaleidoscope. I saw them stand still. They were people. I had sensed them but I could still not discern faces or limbs.

-Aunt Alice said she'd show me later- this much I must have verbalised for Baba said, with a touch of fear and pleasure :

-Did she?-

With that I must have dozed for I felt the light on my pupils and woke to find Baba disappearing into the glow of the electric bulb, a fleeting glimpse of Nancy's transfiguration. The light went out. It was no longer needed for the babyish glow of natural light was coming through the banana leaves. Morning had broken. I was no longer alone. Baba had settled me in with my people.

So whenever you see the Nancy-like filament in the light bulb take care of it. It can light you to the morning. Brer Nancy in a kumbla but he still has power, to show you the way.

Ten

I won't forget the day when the base of the spying glass scratched my bottom. Every time I look in the mirror and see my premature grey hairs, I remember. Every time I see the stretch stripes on my bottom, I feel the pinch again.

Alice was sitting with me at the watering hole, urging me to:

-Try it, try it, try it nuh. Close your eyes. You are a passage, a clean rubber tube. Let the smoke fill you, purify you and kick. The nicest thing you'll ever feel and just kick your feet.-

Well, so what. Why not!

I was a rubber tube floating evenly, deeply, falling through layers of atmosphere, cool and mossy, no cobwebs. Just cool and mossy. Falling evenly, evenly, at six foot catchments. Just deep floating sleep, sleep floating deep, Horlicks sleep, floating evenly deep, ooohs and ouches into a choir of warm, lyric sopranos singing:

-Coming, coming- out of the Jasper walls. I knew they were telling me. My kinsmen came out of the rocks, tall, proud and happy to meet me.

The stalagmites and stalagtites turned into people. Like one-bubby Susan rising out of her graven image. I saw my mother calm as ever leaning on my father's shoulder and saying to me:

-What happen?- in her quick mezzo-soprano voice. I wasn't sure that something had happened. I just knew that I was lying with them like Sunday mornings in the long ago and it was nice. As if she had given a cue, others came. Puppa, my father Alexander's obscure father, black, squat, with a thin bent brown woman looking adoringly at him and saying:

-What happen?-

There was Granny Tucker too and her Corpie, holding hands and her father who had said her blessing would flow like a river. There was great grandfather Will too. White, smiling with both his hands resting on the shoulders of a fidgety, thin black woman who must have been the wife whom the stories claim remarried badly and lost the family fortune. There were scores behind them popping up, popping up like geometric progression or the Gordon's ad. . . . 'You see not one piper but one hundred'. And so it was. Everybody playing the same note:

-What happen?-

It was art from any angle . . . music, shape, production, performance, colour scheme, blending of colours, a pageant. They broke into sections as often in choral speaking:

-Have you seen Locksely, Letitia's boy?-

-Have you seen Uroy, B's son by Stanley's boy?-

-What is Uriah doing with himself?-

-Did Teena really name the child Obadiah after me?-

Names all familiar but I couldn't put faces to them. I wasn't in touch. I couldn't see well enough yet.

-She isn't in touch. She isn't in touch. She can't see well enough yet- Like Gilbert and Sullivan, a conductor-less orchestra, as the contralto, soprano, bass ride the nonsensical chorus:

-She isn't in touch. She isn't in touch. She can't see well enough yet- I wasn't in touch. I was looking at the splendour of it all.

Then a tall one in the back spoke rather than sang:

-I hear they no longer make banana mullum-

Banana mullum. What's banana mullum, I was thinking when the whole chorus softly, then rising to a crescendo, sang:

-What's banana mullum. She don't know banana mullum- They just about used my exact words. They weren't just putting on a performance for me. They were trying

79

to communicate. They were picking their way through my brains. I listened.

I knew banana but not mullum.

-She knows banana but not mullum.-

My mother sang that aria in the clear, clean notes of my childhood :

-Angels of Light, singing to welcome the pilgrims of the night.- It quivered my heart but I thought inappropriately : Mama's voice does not synchronise with the drum. My father sang as if in response :

-When did we only have drums?- and I remembered sitting by my mother's stool and touching the sister notes as she played. I could feel the notes falling under my fingers : I had betrayed them. I remembered Corpie's termite ridden organ passed on to the one that had showed promise, put in a space meant to hold a teacher's diploma. I remembered the struggle to keep it alive, to keep the tongue and the bellows stretching from Corpie to us and I felt that I had betrayed them.

But as if to reassure me, my great-grandmother by my father's side, great grandfather Will's fidgety, unfortunate wife, began to beat the kettle drum and my cousin in the distance, some brother's son perhaps, to blow the bamboo sax. It all fitted in.

It was my time to ask questions now. They played the whole reel again for me, questions and answers. I saw that I only had half of the questions and answers and they the other half. I saw that if I knew all my kin . . . Obadiah, Teena, Locksely, Uroy, I could no longer roam as a stranger; that I had to know them to know what I was about; that I could no how wear my rightful Easter dress, sit in my granny's parlour, eat my cane nor walk in my beautiful garden unless I walked with them, the black and squat, the thin and wizened, all of them.

It was then that I accused them in my mind of contra-

dictory behaviour : of singing a song of unity yet master-
minding our drift apart and in the finale, all blending,
they sang :

-We did our part. Blessings on yours-

I wanted to ask how but they had left and I was
covered from head to toe with dripping water, hot and cold
in perspiration, my hair grey and those funny stripes on
my behind.

INTO THIS BEAUTIFUL GARDEN

Percy the chick trumpeted out "Wake up, Wake up".
Alexander Richmond does not want to wake up leave the
warmth of Sarah Richmond. He shuffles down towards the
bed foot, pulls up his knees and tucks his head under
Sarah's arm. The coir mattress whispers.

Lil flutters from her chocolate tree roost and cackles to
Percy's trumpet "See I am up. See I am up". Sarah Richmond nestles Alexander Richmond's head and touches
her lips to his forehead. She does not want to get up. The
bed is sweet. Alexander Richmond holds his lawful wedded
wife Sarah Richmond tighter and Sarah stiffens. Which
was that one yawning himself awake? Leaford Alfred,
Gladys Maud, Joseph Obediah, William Alexander, Nellie
or Little Rupie.

The bed is sweet and so is Alexander Richmond . . .
sometimes but coir sure can cry and there are already six
children to be brought up in the sight of the Lord. Ham
saw his father's nakedness and was banished. Sarah Richmond is always sweet but coir sure can make noise and
there are already six mouths to feed.

Alexander Richmond hitched up his pants, threw his
feet over his side of the bed, felt for his long boots, felt
for his socks in his boots, and pulled them over his toes and
heels, thrust his foot into his boots and pulled, first one
then the other. Reached up his hand for his shirt from his
nail, and fighting to get both arms in at once, he cleared
his throat in a coughing way and made for outside to
bathe his face in the dew.

Sarah Richmond says "Shh" as she does every morning
except Sunday morning as she pulls the string of her under-
skirt tightly about her waist. Alexander Richmond's walking would have wakened the dead, should have wakened
every one in the room and hall . . . the boards have a
funny way of vibrating with his every step, yet every morning except Sunday morning, Sarah Richmond, pulling her

85

skirt from the two children nearest her foot, tosses as she drags :

-Sister, Nellie, oonoo wake up dem other one. I don't know why these children so hard to wake and they know is short day.-

By chance it is early December.

I am Nellie and I am eight.

* * *

Granny Tucker prayed on Sunday mornings. In truth she always prays. Kneading her bread, she prays for health and strength to continue making bread to supply to the shops, to bring in money to pay Brother Jack to run the sugar mill to make sugar to feed the district. Granny Tucker prays for those who cannot afford to buy bread, for those who sing rag songs and stray from the good book, waste their money on cock fights and cannot buy their bread. She prays for rain to moist the cabbage suckers. She prays that rain will stay away from the ripening tomato field. She prays for Parson Blair and the whole church militant. She prays constantly against Ole Joe, the devil who can tempt you, who can hide one foot of shoes and have you hunting for the other, who can cause your dough to fall.

Granny Tucker prays for the whole community. Give us faith O Lord. Faith in our curing and sustaining power. Faith Dear God, not to fight evil with evil, to stand proud but not so proud that we insult you. Help us to beat down the disruptive force of the Tempter. Nowhere as in us dear God does evil have more sway. And you know why O Lord (and she shakes her head). She prays for Tanny Stewart. Beating graves to get one square of land, to take that foolish woman from his brother, setting springe for that insipid khaki woman. Foolishness. What does it profit you to gain the world and lose your soul! And now facing

86

the pearly gates, confessing to have known the devil.
Stupid Fool. Lord take his tongue.

She prayed constantly. For evil is strong and only with
God can it be fought.

But on Sunday mornings Granny Tucker prays especially
for her children dispersed to the ends of the world . . . three,
eight, forty miles and even overseas doing what she does
not know but God knows best. On Sunday mornings,
Granny Tucker rouses at Sheila's bark, rubs her eyes, says
"Praise God for another day", breathes in heavily and
says "Praise God" again, and like an alto sax tuning up or
an organ finding the prelude to an anthem, she hums . . .
just notes in different keys and octaves, sometimes in her
chest, sometimes in her throat, sometimes with lips apart,
eventually into song with words :

> Jesus still lead on
> Til our rest be won
> And although the way be cheerless
> We will follow calm and fearless.

Yes Lord, feed her spirit.

On Sunday mornings Granny Tucker prays on her knees,
hands clasped and resting on her bed, knees joined to that
vast expanse of dark, shine, broad, breadfruit wood, she
prays for the six children 'you put in this house'. She
prays for them by order of birth.

Granny prays for Eliza married before her time, married
yes Lord but to a sinner. Touch his heart Lord if only for
my chile's sake. Take away the rum and the dice. Hold his
hand and steady him Lord. Keep your hand on him and
mek we hold up our head.

She prays for Rita. In Colon. But you know best Lord.
Keep her close to your feet and show her the way. I don't
hear nothing Lord but keep her straight. Keep her from

87

the pomp and vanity of this wicked world. Keep her from lip rouge and straighten hair. Take her hand Lord and keep her on the straight and narrow.

And Naomi. Only you dear Lord know why you take her in the prime of her life and leave these two little ones motherless and fatherless. Dear Jesus, show me how to keep them in the fold for I don't young again and you know it.

She prays for the boys. Don't strike me Lord, if I pray a little harder for my boy children, Lord. Is them must keep the name. Is them belong at your right hand. Bring them back Lord. Bring them back. I not kneeling down here for nothing. I don't go to church every Sunday for nothing. Bring them back Lord. You know I need them. Me one can't carry on. Brother Jack help. I thank you Lord. But blood thicker than water. What them doing in that wicked city. Can't even hear from them. Who to knock a nail if you want it knock. My hand weak now. Show them the joy of looking up into their mother eye. I stay with my father and get the blessing. Tell them what it is like.

You didn't bring Albert from the dead to work in no cock-fighting pit? You same one did give me a hard time with Obediah, Lord and it have to have some meaning. I not questioning you Lord, but what is this putting out, putting out to sea that he always writing to tell me 'bout? That just don't sound right Lord. Not even one of them you don't give a nose for your ministry; Lord!

Carlton is here Lord. Is it he? But he say he is going Lord and I can't stop in his way. Then who going to carry your cross?

It is Sarah's time.

-I have a wash belly Dear Saviour. You know it. You gave her to me. Didn't even get to see the father. Sarah is the name. I pick out teacher for her but you didn't want that for her. You turn her woman. You give her Alexander Richmond and two acres of land and six mouths to feed . . . Leaford Alfred, Gladys Maud, Joseph Obediah, William Alexander, Nellie, Rupie and the one she say coming. Pardon me Lord, those sneaking khaki people wouldn't let my chile rest. Every year so! I am only woman Lord and I beg you guide me for I can't question you. I can only say "Take the case Lord. Take the case for is your case". So take the case, Lord.-

Granny Tucker sighs and makes to rise, half mumbling: -You give me good man but you take him soon. Keep me Corpie good-

Eyes glazed and far away, Granny Tucker takes her hands from her nightdress and lets it fall to her hips; takes her stays from her bed head and hunches her shoulders, now one now the other as she pushes her arms through the openings. Lifts one, now the other breast, as she fits them into their sockets. From under her pillow, she takes her small clothes, a baggy affair, steps in and with her hand under her nightdress, pulls the string hard around her waist. She lets the dress slip to her feet and steps out of it; pulls her flannel merino over her head, ties her petticoat around her waist and hooks the bodice over this, smoothing out the bulges, the while. Then she takes her day frock from the rack, pulls it over her head, hooks the press-stud at the side and reaches for her tie-head all the while singing and humming "Guide me O thou great Jehovah" as if in her toilet too she needs His guiding hand.

-Ham laughed at his father and was banished. You have to grow the children in the sight of the Lord- Granny mutters.

-Janey and Lou. Come over. It is time to pray-

-The children must be brought up in the sight of the Lord- Granny mutters.

Granny Tucker gets to her knees again with her granddaughters on either side :

-Lord defend this thy child and this thy child- she pats them on the head.

-Gentle Jesus meek and mild . . . go on Janey go on . . . Louise who you going to pray for?-

-You Granny-

-Not me one Lou. Pray for your aunts and your uncles. Pray for Aunt Sarah and her house. Call everybody by name. Say it now. God bless Aunt Sarah, bless Leaford Alfred, bless Gladys Maud, bless Joseph Obediah, bless William Alexander, bless your play mate Nellie and little Rupie. You too Jane. Pray for each other. Pray to God to make you good girls-

-Mustn't pray for Uncle Alexander too-

-You know that Louise, you know that. Who else you going to pray for?-

-Everybody Granny-

-Not yet. Anybody else special?-

-Don't know Granny-

-Who you know that dying chile?-

-Mass Tanny Granny-

-Yes Mass Tanny. Pray that he reach the mercy seat. Pray that your grandfather and your mother and father stay there. They were good people. You come from good stock. Don't mind the evil 'round you. You must be proud and thankful for that.-

The cool Christmas breeze is blowing.

-Put on your sweater. Wash your face and rinse your mouth and look after the chuunies-

The teasing Christmas breeze is blowing. It is early December and they too are eight.

* * *

-Dear Lord as I Rebecca Pinnock do venture to approach thy mercy seat where thou art wont to answer prayer, look down upon the sick and afflicted. Look down upon Tanny Stewart, Lord take his tongue . . .-

We children had heard about it but we didn't quite believe it. What was our Aunt Becca doing in Mass Mehiah's thatch church praying? Children could go and sing and clap and even take part in the King and Queen show but our big people . . . no. Our big people could go as guests but when they prayed, they prayed in our church with its bell and organ. When our big people prayed in church, they said the same thing altogether from prayer books. Things like Our Father . . . and I believe. . . . And they don't testify. So what is Aunt Becca doing there.

Mama and Papa knew of it. We sensed that. They knew why too but Mama only said:

-Hog pickney ask him mek him mout so long. Hog say "you a grow you wi see"- which meant that we would never hear a word of it from her. Papa pretended we hadn't spoken and Aunt Alice just smiled.

Why was Aunt Becca of all people praying in Mass Mehiah's church and for Mass Tanny? Why was Aunt Becca praying so hard for Mass Tanny in Mass Mehiah's church when she lives in the teacher's cottage right next to the church where our big people pray?

Aunt Becca Pinnock is short and stout. Not like great grandfather Will or like Alexander Richmond her brother. But Aunt Becca has the colour. Only Aunt Becca took great grandfather's colour.

Aunt Becca is brown. She lives in the Teacher's cottage, plays for church and teaches Sunday school. Aunt Becca came out the best. Aunt Becca used to teach. Aunt Becca married Teacher. Teacher Pinnock. So why is Aunt Becca

91

praying for Mass Tanny in Mass Mehiah's bamboo and thatch church when our big people's church is in her back yard?

Errol and Barry are something to Teacher and live in the cottage too. They know what Aunt Becca is doing but they don't know why. Teacher says that he has never seen her going and never seen her there so he does not know that Aunt Becca is praying for Mass Tanny in Mass Mehiah's thatch and bamboo church.

Aunt Becca is my father's eldest sister. Eldest child is fair of face. Aunt Becca is a lady. Aunt Becca is a lady who feels shame. Plenty of shame. But mostly for her family. Aunt Alice shames her. Aunt Alice has no husband. Aunt Alice works nowhere. She never seems to make a living. She plants nothing. She reaps nothing but only helps us now and again, helps out Aunt Becca now and again and smiles. Aunt Alice in Wonderland. Aunt Alice is so nice.

I have shamed Aunt Becca and will shame Aunt Becca. My mother has so many children. I told the new pink parson that my name was N . . . (Is that not what it said: "What is your name, N or M". Well my name is N) Aunt Becca is ashamed that I will fail the parish scholarship. Aunt Becca wishes that I would follow Egbert around less. It shames Aunt Becca that I sit with him while he cooks the hog's food. It shames her past all understanding to know that I eat the cooked breadfruit hearts meant for his hog. Hoity toity Aunt Becca with her stockings bumped under her knee.

And this is Aunt Becca who is praying in Brer Mehiah's bamboo and thatch church. What has come over Aunt Becca, that little brown dog sniffing out things that will shame her!

Aunt Becca's shaming eye ruled our roost. Aunt Becca's

92

crinkly hair scooped away from her face, stuck out in a point barely touching the top of her shoulder like a fish tail in a trapped hair net. Aunt Becca's tiny feet in her pomps. Aunt Becca's round brown self, her thin lips pursed together like a shrivelled star apple. Aunt Becca's fish eyes shamed everyone into unworthiness.

Alexander Richmond was ashamed that he liked to wash his face in dew, that he still believed that dew water was as good as any doctor's lotion. He had so many children; his house was so small there was hardly anywhere in it for them to sit. He was generally ashamed. All his children clamped up like shama macca at one step of Aunt Becca's pomps. That shamed him. Sarah Richmond was ashamed that she had married Mrs Becca Pinnock's brother rather than finish her exams; that she had given him so many children and the wash belly she was carrying 'at this stage of her life' aborted itself at Aunt Becca's coming.

Aunt Becca walked into our lives through the mekke-mekke of late December; through bits of balloon beaten into mud, through soggy bits of crepe paper and paste, picking her little brown dog way into the warmth of our house.

Our Aunt Becca was the new teacher's wife and one glance from her turned little Rupie's diapers hanging across the hall into old rags handed down from Leaford Alfred to Gladys Maud to Joseph Obediah to William Alexander and to me; turned the hall and all of us into the nasty bits of crepe paper and burst balloons from which our house had sheltered us. Aunt Becca was all cleanness and decency.

So how come Aunt Becca sat on those bamboo benches surrounded by perspiration, drum beat and moaning.

* * *

Aunt Becca did not scare Janey and Louise nor for that

93

matter Teacher Pinnock and Janey and Louise knew why. They knew that Aunt Becca was khaki. Now what did that mean? For us it meant drudging clothes. For them it meant well . . . khaki! And that settled the matter for them. Besides she is sneaking khaki and they knew that Teacher Pinnock knew. Well!! Aunt Becca must have known that they knew. She kept her interfering eye on other things when they came to stay. Their visits were much too short. Granny Tucker was much too sure that the Richmond house could not hold two extra bodies for more than two weeks and that they might starve when the food she sent ran out. Janey and Louise's visits freed up everybody. Aunt Alice especially. They gave tongue to her smiles. They were tongue to her thoughts.

In Teacher Pinnock's first year, we were all eight. It was in the April of that year that Aunt Becca gave me that bag for my birthday and made me miss my lines. Janey and Louise came to stay for the first time in the mid-summer of that year. It was that same mid-summer that had Aunt Becca sneaking into Mass Mehiah's church.

Alexander Richmond does not leave his house on Sunday mornings. Instead of pulling on his socks and shoes and stomping out to wash his face, he shakes Sarah Richmond as he sits up on his side of the bed, dressed except for his shoes and socks.

-Sarah call the children- he says and Sarah calls the children.

My father Alexander has a democratic way. Every Sunday he opens the floor. Anyone who wishes to, can offer a prayer aloud. We rarely offer. Kneeling with our heads on our parents' double bed is enough. Having no water to carry and no wood to fetch is a treat. Anticipating the smell of polished shoes, clean, starched good dresses is enough for us. But that Sunday morning, Janey, one of the little ones wanted to pray aloud. Wanted to offer a prayer for Mass Tanny, that his soul rest in peace. Now where did she get that?

-And that he stop confessing to things he couldn't have done-

My father snuffed out a lighted squib.

-Yes let us pray for all dying men for you will soon understand that all life must come eventually to dying like your grandfather and your Uncle Lester and your Aunt Dorcas and your parents Janey-

And that was that. They let the matter rest. With those twins you simply had to wait until they were ready to talk. No buttering up, no bribing, no special piece of food could let them open their mouths.

It was Teacher Pinnock's sermon that did it.

-When her smiles failed, her tears prevailed-

He was talking about Delilah and the whole church was quiet. You could know that this was going to be one of those times when big people would crowd around him and say:

-You touched me today Teacher- and Aunt Becca would smile as if they were addressing her.

-When her smiles failed . . .-

Louise staring straight at Teacher Pinnock said to me under her breath: -Mass Tanny is confessing that he killed your Uncle Lester and lots of people and kept his brother Stanley down because she would not marry him-

-She who?-

-Miss Khaki-

-Marry whom-

-Mass Tanny-

So what is this now. We knew that Mass Tanny and

Mass Stanley were related but didn't know how. We knew that Mass Tanny had done something to Uncle Lester but Aunt Becca was to marry him! What is this now?

-So why is she going to Mass Mehiah's church to pray for him?-

-Guilty. She is guilty and you all are family-

-We related to Mass Tanny and Mass Stanley?-

Louise shuffled and began to listen intently to the rest of Teacher's sermon. She had burst her squib and was finished. She had turned off as tightly as our broken standpipe cock. I would get no more.

But our minds hatched and set and hatched and multiplied like fleas and chiggers. Like the time we learnt of sex and babies:

-You remember the time when Mama and Papa did bathe in the same pan? Hmmm that's why. That's why her belly did get so big-

-That is not true for she would have did have a baby-

Any bit of information that hinged even slightly on the theme was priceless. We bargained for information, we blackmailed, we peeped:

-If you tell me what you did see on the sheet, I will tell you what Girlie tell me-

-OK then. I will tell you but you must tell me first-

-No Sir. You first for Girlie have a baby already and what I know is more than what you know-

-Well then, I did see blood on the sheet and that mean say . . .-

-All right then, I will tell you. Girlie say is like when your mother have a bottle of honey and she say nobody must touch it. And everybody tief out some but is only you one get catch-

-Oh that is honey moon-

-And she say that she did think that is bad stomach she

96

did have and she was taking castor oil for it but her baby father box the glass out of her hand and she never get to drink it and her father kick her with his water boots and run her out of the house-

Uhhhmmmm. That is that. If there is more, we a grow, we will see. And we allowed another mystery to seduce us.

Now what did Janey and Louise mean? They weren't too cold either for our big people were fidgeting.

-How do they know so much- they were saying but we knew that. We knew that Granny prayed in great detail and loudly. Besides, the partition between their room and hers was very low and they could see and hear anything she did or said. In any case Granny Tucker talked aloud to herself all the time.

Any scrap of news about Aunt Becca and Mass Tanny, Mass Stanley and how and why they were related to us, was tucked away in our unconscious waiting for the other pieces to fit the jigsaw puzzle.

Aunt Alice knew that we wanted to know but she only smiled and when we pestered her too much, she sang:

> Jane and Louisa will soon come home
> Into this beautiful garden.

And that was that.

* * *

Every first of August at about three o'clock Papa Son's bamboo sax bellows out:

> Cum awf a Mattie belly . . .

Oh Jeezaz and I can't get my hair plait fast enough to answer the call.

> Cum awf a Mattie belly . . . ly
> Far Mattie belly is so saaf and tender

> Cum awf a Mattie belly . . .

and it makes your skin itch and makes you feel as if you
want to wee-wee and you can't even tell anybody how you
feel. You are just miserable because you are not there
yet . . .

> Far Mattie belly is a engine rubber
> Cum awf a Mattie belly . . .

If is not Papa Son, is Kissie Dover. And if it is not Mattie
Belly is Peanut Vendor but it still don't matter for is still
the same bamboo alto sax. And is the same church fair
ground. With the coconut bough shed bigger than anything
you ever see. A platform in the middle for the musicians
and booths, bamboo enclosures for stalls. Snowball man,
fresco man, pattie pan man, toto woman, drops . . .
everything but nothing like Kissie or Papa Son standing up
straight and pushing out his chest like a cock trying to
crow and stretching as if to put the horn through the
coconut boughs . . .

> Cum awf a Mattie belly . . .

You can see it even if you're not there yet. You putting
on your shoes with the cross straps, your patent leather
shoes you've been vaselin-ing for days, your organdy dress
with puff sleeves and your socks to match. Your big fat
hair ribbon sticking off a mile. Your straw handbag and
your 'kerchief in your hand still wet at the corner from
the nine-pence bottle of khus-khus water which your uncles
in Town send you every now and then.

But you're not speaking to anyone for they will not
come on and the man is saying :

> Cum awf a Mattie belly

and you just left to cry. And you can't go by yourself for
Sister have the tickets and all the spending money and

though Mass Stanley know you from the day you were born, this is a business day and the church needs the money for the foreign ministry and everybody must present a ticket so they won't let me in.

Pi pananana Pi pananana pananana a dududups dup-dups. And you know that a circle has gathered around Miss P and whoever her partner is, that she has just finished trembling her belly and that her partner has just done pushing his leg between her two to signify the end of the dance and you weren't there to see it.

For what seems like centuries, Mass Stanley has kept the fair gate. He does not belong to our church but he has travelled and knows all kinds of behaviours so nobody dares fool with him . . . stranger or district people. So he is the best man to keep the gate. Mass Stanley is round and very black. Everything about him is round. His belly, himself, his chest, his nose, his mouth. His face and head form a round commander coco with valleys dug out for eyes and top lip. His eyes are all brown, pupil and iris are all the same. You don't see him. He doesn't see you. You just see the sparkle like a peeny wally shining by day or by night. He is a favourite of mine and I am a favourite of his. He is the tar baby that cut Nanny Goat down to size. And it more than pleases me that this tar baby and I have a way with each other. I have his ticket, he says and I feel that I can do anything with him except go through that fair gate and up the hill to the fair ground without paying.

My Mass Stanley pleases me most at the last part of the Fair, when he is no longer the gate man but my Mass Stanley. He appears on the Fair Ground. Coming up the hill, under the booth now, the most brilliant peeny wally, and everybody feels him, although jam packing one another, they should be locked down in their own steps. Mass Stanley is coming; it is ten o'clock in the night and late for lesser ones like me. Kissie and Papa Son and everybody know. Is Mass Stanley time now and I know that Aunt Becca woulda give her eye teeth to partner him in the quadrille but he has never danced with anyone else but Miss Elsada. Only when she says:

-Cho Stan, dance with somebody else this time- and she calls out somebody's name. But that hardly ever happens.

Ten o'clock is Mass Stanley's time and the whole Fair Ground knows this. Peanut man O, Patti pan O, be he Papa Son or Kissie Dover. And I am full of pride. Silence. Mass Stanley in his cut away coat, his panama straw hat with the pin-prick holes, his two-toned shoes with their pin-pricked holes. Mass Stanley O. And Miss Sada in her peplum dress and her upsweep hair. There are others too but they don't matter. If Alexander Richmond was there now, it would be different but my father doesn't dance.

Silence.

You hear me.

Is banjo man time now and old man time now.

Mass John get up like him young and like him been Kissie Dover and Papa Son all day. He hug up that banjo with its white basin and sway her and drag his finger backs against the strings and you 'fraid to draw your breath as the old people stand up like buckram in a bottle, man holding woman round her waist like we never see in ordinary life. She looking up at him like she beautiful and slim and she in the view master machine. Man leaning his head and looking down at his partner like he do that

100

every day for the last century.

And they start.

Watch them leaning stiff like starch. O Mass Stanley!
Look how him fling him foot from the knee and stick it
off like him slim. O Mass Stanley. Again. Quiet there.
Again. Watch Mass Stanley foot! Second figure now.

Rock the lady. Rock the lady on your toes. Walk like
you going somewhere and yet is only behind her and
around to come right back to your space. With one hand
behind your back, kick the knee and stick out the heel. O
Mass Stanley, toe it. She to the right and you to the left
and let that square of a shoe box into a parallelogram
and back. O. Look at her cross your shoulder. She pretty
eh and she so light and is only Miss Rose in her coarse
boots tomorrow. Bring her round. That's right and keep
your hand round her til she stand in place and the music
stop. Right.

Third figure now and everybody is a soldier and the
ladies are waving them off to war. Yes now Charlie, let
we hear the rhumba box. We hear it. Now send off the
men ladies, send them off. Let them work. Mass Stanley
worked in foreign, served in the war so he knows. Right
men. Go on by yourselves. Go on. Show off. Hold up your
head and smell. Smell him. You better than him but is
all right. Yes move round him and let him know that you
know but is still all right. You don't hold it 'gainst him. And
come back to your women now. Send them up to warm up.
Let them know each other. Give them their chance but
show them how. That's right. Bow to each other. Mannersable. That's right. Show them your rhythm Miss Lou
but gently, that's right. Decent and gentle. Now smell them.
See who have on what but be mannersable. Greet them.
Let them feel at home but let them know that you are still

101

the best and you know it. Go back to your man and tell him is all right. All of you come together now and say is all right. Is all right. It hot and sweaty but is still all right. Is all right now Charlie. Tie up the rhythm.

Yes.

Cutting wood. You mad now and we understand.

Figure Four. Beat the box Charlie. Rock and stomp. You own the whole world. Rock and stomp. We out here looking but is not we. Is stage audience. Rock and stomp and move off by yourself. Mass Stanley I can depend on you. Slide out by yourself with your back foot. Turn round, kick your leg from the knee and stick out your heel. O Mass Stanley. Find Miss Sada now and lead her out and mek we see her dance. But you not craven. You not selfish. You know how to treat other women even if they not nice like Miss Elsada. Take in the other man wife. Take her in sir. Take her in. Show her courtesy. Lead her up to the rest and introduce her. Miss Sada don't mind. Let her meet Miss Sada. Now take them both in so everybody know that nothing not going on behind her back. Take her. O yes Sir. Yes Mass Stanley. But you can take your medicine. See the other man coming for Miss Sada. Yes. Don't vex. Bow to him nicely. Yes Sir. Mek him know is all right for you did take his wife for a dance too. Smile Sir. He doing well but he can't do well like you. No sir. Miss Elsada know it and the other lady know it too but they trying with the other man. They polite; they don't want him to know. And you polite too, you wouldn't want him to know either but all of we know. Smile sir. She coming back now. Cool off. Simmer down. Give it to Mass John and the banjo. Him is older man, let him simmer it down. Yes Mass John, they need you. Slap your hand back, flash your fingers. Give them pause to let them know that they must simmer down. Flash again and again and stop.

Figure five.

One, two, three pause.
When cow 'kin done.
Ah wey Harry a go do. . . .
Anything goes. Do the lancers. Slide, slide and hop then
kimbo and stick; slide, slide and hop, then kimbo and stick.
Slide, slide and hop, then kimbo and stick. . . .

* * *

I loved Mass Stanley and nobody seemed to mind. There
were pimento trees in his yard growing out of rocks. And
the rocks were peculiar too. They were full of holes. You
had to walk carefully for if you stubbed your toe, it was
liable to get stuck and to break off altogether. And the
rocks had a smell. Sometimes of coffee and tobacco and
sometimes of sweet soap as if Miss Sada washed them.
Seems to me though that if she put coffee water or kananga
water or any such thing in them to give them that smell,
those cupped stones would harbour mosquitoes and it didn't
seem that Mass Stanley and Miss Sada had any more
mosquitoes than we had. So I don't know how come their
yard smelt so sweet.

They liked to have me creeping into their house too. I
would walk in and sit at the doorway and Mass Stanley,
smoking his pipe in his rocking chair by the door, would
crinkle his eyes and start talking to me. Or sometimes, he
would say: "You know Elsada" or "You know Baba"
and I knew that it was me he was talking to for they had
all been there before me and he hadn't said a thing to
them. He had been rocking and smoking and thinking and
because I came, he got brave enough to think aloud because
he knew that I wanted to know. He told me about Cuba
and cutting canes and driving ox-driven carts, about fruto-
pan and fighting in Cuba and Belgium. Mass Stanley had
lived.

He told me about Manalva and how the district was.

103

And how he used to ride a horse with his sword and shield to protect the queen.

-And a bet you couldn't tell me who was the queen eh girl?-

And I would guess and guess. -No you couldn't know. Who now would know what Coolie Gal used to be like-

And I still didn't know.

-Mammy Cool. Coolie Gal. A lovely samba girl every man wanted. Something like your Aunt Becca-

And every time Miss Sada would say:

-You have to bring Rebecca een? Stan is only a chile you know. Mine you let her grow big before her time-

-Cho Elsada, what that can do?- and he would be side-tracked into some other argument.

-My time now one like this working for herself and looking to find herself a husband before trouble take her. But you not going to have no trouble Nellie. You can fight. So much so that people won't even want to fight you. So you won't even see trouble. But now and again you must try to know it; it can trip you and fall you and you wouldn't even know what hit you for you don't know how trouble stay- He would wink at me and I would smile. There was some meaning there but mi ah grow mi wi see.

At other times he would press on to the end before Miss Sada caught him. -Something like your Aunt Becca but not so stocious. Bwoy she did stocious bad! Fellow Pinnock. Poh! Becca have too much juice for him. She never take her match. Thank God Coolie Gal was big woman to me or else I woulda bruk mi neck two times. Chile, woman sweet-

Janey and Lou were right. There was something to know.

Other times, he was very quiet and Miss Sada would

look at him in a special way as if she was his angel.

I could know as soon as I crept through the under-
growth of coffee trees that separated my father's land from
his house how things were going with Mass Stanley. If he
was in one of those quiet far away dreams, between Miss
Sada and he, they would take away all the sunshine and
the excitement and leave me in a cold, white cloudy
November day without even the sound of rain drops. If
she was in the kitchen, if she was washing outside, if she
was in the hall, it didn't matter. Miss Sada would collect
all the sunshine and the life from everywhere into herself
and she would beam it at him. I would stand outside and
see the light like the sun boring through two shrivelled
shingles. It would come like the enlightening focus of a
flashlight in the dark, beaming straight and constant from
Miss Sada, whether it be her back or her knee or her hand,
coming from whichever part of her that was in direct line
with Mass Stanley's head. I knew I couldn't cross it.

* * *

-You call this ground Sah-

Stanley Ruddock did not answer.

-The cutlass can't even go down much less mi fi go put
fork into this-

-Boy, you know you sinning-

-Sin Sah! Don't is sin fi haffe work dis? Ah punishment
dis sah-

Mass Stanley's coal black face turned blue. Silently he
cut a calabash switch. And just as silently, he jammed his
cutlass in the ground. He switched the switch to his right
hand, flexed it from his wrist to make sure that it was
supple and he laced David. It was shocking.

A fifty year old man cannot beat an eighteen year old
lad. He should have known that and kept his anger. But

105

his Daddy left him nothing. He had cleaned grass for a bit a day. Bought land. Sold it. Went to Cuba, came back and yes made a fool of himself and had started all over again. This was Stanley Ruddock. These two acres of stone at Wood are Stanley Ruddock, the soul that he will pass on to his son and his son's sons and for his one and only child to come and rebuke him about it, to tell him that his life was nothing, he could not take. He knew what the land was. He was not blind, was not an idiot. It was stone but it would damned well have to bear something. This thankless bare-faced child. He must show respect but instead he trying to take the switch from me his father!

Is a fight now between father and son and if that is not a sin now, what is? And stranger have to part us! To come between man and his flesh! What a thankless child!

And the boy keeping malice with his father 'stead of getting down on his knees and asking his forgiveness. He know what he going through? He know what he has gone through! Boy not even out of egg shell good yet! Elsada couldn't stand for this. "Honour thy mother and father that they days may be long in this land" is what the Bible said. David had to go. Her one blessing but he would have to go.

Elsada Ruddock had been born Coretta Psalms but everyone knew her by her home name, Elsada. She was from down the country and like down the country people, was as red as bauxite dirt. The second to last of eleven children all born within wedlock, she had kept herself untouched and seen to it that her little sister, Malvina, kept herself likewise. Had served her mother and father in the sight of God and seen them in their graves before she and her charge ventured out with the school teacher and his family to these parts.

Elsada had seen Stanley Ruddock come home. She

106

had seen him come back from foreign with his gun foot pants, his straw hat and chain and seen him spending money like it was going out of style on uppity Rebecca Richmond who was even then spooning with his brother too. Fancy that.

The man suffer! All she could do was to wash the white drill pants when he asked her to, so that he could look clean to take the Richmond girl to tea meetings and rally and fairs and dancing and what have you. That man suffer!

The woman suck him til him turn saw dust. What kind of work can a rich man just come back from foreign, courting that stocious teacher gal, do? Couldn't go back to saw board like before, couldn't split shingle like before, couldn't clean ground like before?

Yes. He let down Alexander. Alexander wasn't Stanley's playmate . . . was small boy to him but you could see that he looked up to him. Now all of that lost. Psyche and Trim they had been, Elsada had heard, before Stanley left for foreign. Sawing . . . they were there together; cleaning ground . . . they were there together, catching bird, they were there together. . . . He let Alexander down. Alexander try with him. Try with him. So nobody should point finger and say that Alexander sell out the shingle trade under him. No. And Alexander did not set his sister on him. No. I personally see Alexander sit down with Stanley and say:

-Stanley I not going anywhere unless you going with me. No wood not cutting, no board not sawing, no shingle not splitting, unless is you and me- But the man couldn't wait forever. Who could blame him if he sell out and buy land and go off to work on his own. Moonstruck that Stanley. Moonstruck.

All Stanley could do was strum banjo. And for all the foolishness that he was going on with, I did really love that. Yes, he could play the banjo.

Elsada had a pigeon chest and a long high bottom.
These days the peplum really fit her. The frills sat nicely
on her bottom. Those days Stanley only knew that she
was a spirit that understood. Only she knew it when he
struck up a chord. And more and more since Rebecca left,
he would find himself striking up a chord for 'Shango
Bachelor' and waiting to hear Elsada, coming back with
her water from the Spring or cooking in Teacher's kitchen,
responding to him, in a high clear voice like a flute to his
banjo:

> O what a shame, she has lost her name
> Don't know who to blame, making a fame
> With Shango bachelor.

Must be they used to sing it in her parts. It was popular
with his pasajeros but when he came back home nobody
seemed to know it.

When Malvina fall and go clean out of her head, he
felt it for Elsada. Poor Elsada. A stranger in a strange
land and all she had was Malvina. Coretta Elsada Psalms
and her sister Malvina Psalms. And people laughed.
Nothing like that ever happened before and even now
they still talking: "What too good ants eat for them sup-
per". "Tun colour meet him Waterloo." Poor chile. The
Syrian droger never even come back to collect the money
people owed him.

He self help put Malvina in her straight jacket. So he
made a point of stopping 'round Teacher now and again
with his banjo. Poor Elsada, not a God soul in the world.
She need looking after. Poor Stanley, not a God cent left
of his Cuba money. He need looking after. Then Teacher
got the new school at Salt Spring and Stanley told her
not to bother to move with them.

So Stanley take up responsibility now!

108

It was really Elsada who took up the responsibility. Seems she never learnt to say No to it. With government taking care of Malvina and Teacher gone, Elsada needed someone to look after and Stanley would do well. There was so much evil around him. Know-all-nigger had it to say that he had taken away his brother's sweetheart and through shame his brother had turned him into a ne'er-do-well and done him out of the land he had bought with his Cuba money. Elsada would have to build him from scratch.

They built a balance between them. A balance of weights — the Libra sign as in the horoscope book. When one was down, the other mounted up, the better to slide energy along the cross piece to re-ignite the other and restore the balance. It was more often Stanley whose balance needed restoration.

Elsada did not want to send David away. But she knew that she would have to and that she would have to give the order. Two bulls cannot reign in the same pen; two cocks cannot crow in the same yard. Everybody knew that. David was a god-given gift. He was the one. He was not given to Coretta Elsada Ruddock; he was not given to Stanley Ephraim Ruddock. He was given to Mr and Mrs Ruddock, conceived after their union was blessed by the church. He had to fit somewhere along that balancing rod or go. That was how the Lord designed it.

David was Elsada's belly pain. He could not tell him to go. He could not be the accuser and the judge as well. That was too much weight. If it never did happen! If he could only have kept his anger. Is nobody's fault but his own that he let his Cuba money go to his head and that he had to start over again with nothing. That was not really David's fault. But what had happened had happened and it couldn't be undone. David couldn't stay now and it was left to

Elsada to say the word. So Elsada said the word and David went.

-So the boy was feeling his manhood long time- was all she said when they brought the baby to her two weeks after.

-Are these the fruits of a Christian life?- she said aloud, on behalf of Stanley and herself for the benefit of the fallen girl, the fallen parents and the whole district. But Stanley did not need to smile to let Elsada know what he was feeling and she did not need to speak less gruffly of the child, to let him know that she too knew, that God was still in his Heaven and that He was still smiling.

* * *

On those days when Mass Stanley was not remembering things that he did not want to remember and when Miss Sada was not balancing that rod of light, I could go any-where in the atmosphere. Yet I hardly met Baba. He was a little older than me and in a higher class than me. He had a bulla cake brown skin that was very smooth. It had no cuts — seemed he never had a sore-foot. He was always playing by himself. He had toys. A doctor's kit, a carpenter set. He would measure water and set down the answer in a book. It seems he never ever was around to hear Mass Stanley's stories and he never got in the way of his grand-parents' telegraph wires. He never disturbed their balance.

I did not particularly like Baba. I don't think that Barry or Errol really liked him either. Egbert, he of course would hardly see! He played with us, you know and would even show us what he was doing. But he was a balloon punc-turer. He had no taste for mystery. He didn't know how to stretch out a story and tempt you. Make you light, then make you heavy. Make you frightened, then make you giggle. He always knew the end and told it. Besides, be-

cause of him, I could never profit on the stories Mass
Stanley told me. If I should say: "One time in Cuba such
and such", people would say:

-Where did you get that?- and I would have to say:

-From Mass Stanley- and everybody would know that he
was Baba's grandfather and that if anybody had a right
to tell his stories, it was Baba. But he never did so and I
had to watch opportunities for conversation and status go
by and sit on a store of knowledge all by myself.

Baba was a big people's boy. They loved him. They said
that he made their hearts full. They warned Miss Sada to
look about him:

-Remember Stanley's sister Phyllis?- even those who could
not have known her were saying. Miss Sada had not known
her but she had heard the story a million times.

-Phyllis was growing nicely. Just like Baba there. Pass
her first year exam and everything and bad-minded people
cut down the child in her youth. They can give him all
kinds of things you know Miss Sada. Don't make him eat
from schoolchildren. Harmless as you see them there, they
will put poison in banana and egg and give it to him. I
know what I saying. Phyllis lovely hair drop off clean,
clean before she dead. Is the saw dust and butter rolled up
in the banana-

Miss Sada had to roll her eyes up to heaven so that her
handkerchief-head-scarf rested on her back. She had to
open her arms wide and lift them up to heaven and let her
skirt tail sway a little. She had to sigh heavily: -Look to
Jesus, Miss Amy (or Miss B or Miss whoever). And thank
God that he send a messenger like you to give us the
warning-

Miss Sada never told them that she had seen enough
evil in her life time and fought with enough evil to know

111

it face to face. People had a great deal of strength and power in their hearts; they wanted to use it kindly for you, but like damned up water, it had no morals: it could as easily be let towards you as against you. No higher deity than a snob gave it its direction. The minute our people felt that you slighted their powers, they turned evil and all the force in their hearts would be channelled into making their evil warnings come true. There are and were in every age, in every group and in every place, Miss Sada knew, certain rituals needed to stay the power of this evil. She must prostrate herself to the prophets. Miss Sada knew the prostrating stance and she performed it every time. Roll up your eyes to heaven, spread-eagled style, sway your skirt tail and sigh helplessly.

And they continued to come. When inspector noticed Baba and made much of him, they came:

-You don't come from here and you think you live here long enough to know but you are still a stranger. These district people are wicked. Remember is not so long ago that inspector notice Dotty and look what happen to her. Set the chile own grand uncle on her and turn her fool. Look 'bout Baba before it too late — Miss Sada would prostrate herself and thank the messenger.

God had taken one and he had sent another to replace him. That was God. Not a thing would happen to Baba if only she could tap their strength, and power and kindness and prostrate herself.

Even Aunt Becca liked Baba but she never said more than:

-That boy is sent here for a purpose-.

I remember that day how he shocked her.

Miss Sada had said, or so we heard, that she wasn't going to let anybody dis-crim-in-ate against him and bap-

tise him after everybody else's children. So he had been
blessed at the Baptist church instead of being christened
like the rest of us and he did not come to our Sunday
School so Aunt Becca did not know him. She noticed him
at the harvest rally.

Every first Sunday in September, we have harvest at our
Church. Our church is set in far from the road, upon a
little mound. It is oblong and sits snug upon the hill like a
broad belt atop a flaired skirt. The church is cool and quiet
and carries no sound at all. You can't even hear the
board and the zinc snapping under the sun. Seems the
sun does not bother it at all. Every Saturday evening, the
girls' brigade sit in the vestry and clean the brass whether
tomorrow is Parson's Sunday or not. Cleanliness is next
to Godliness. The Saturday before harvest is different.
Boys are here too and men and women. Bringing long
white salango canes, bunches of coconuts, bunches of grape-
fruits and tangerines, dried chocolates, bissy, eggs, fat long
yams, potatoes, grater cakes, little sewn-up dresses, rugs.
Mass Stanley helps us on these days. He makes an arch of
plaited coconut boughs at each door, ties bunches of grape-
fruits, tangerines, oranges, one at the top and one at each
side of each door. He decorates the benches. Our benches
have shoulders with a heart-shaped hole in each as if God
forgot to put an arm there. Mass Stanley with Bada Reg
and his wife Love-up finish these arms with strings of
onions, tangerines, sweet potatoes in all kinds of colours.
Where plaques to dead relatives were driven into the walls,
we have hanging bunches of bananas.

The younger bodies must decorate the pulpit, the altar
and the lectern. They are now masses and masses of ferns
with roses, stinking pretty, forget-me-nots and late June
roses. The church is not only still : it is a cool still garden.
And even Aunt Becca's sounds at the organ do not disturb
it :

113

-Let us go it through one more time . . . You can't see. Well let us borrow some of the candles just this one time.-

Teacher, Melvin, Busha, Miss Amy, Aunt Saar, Miss Vera, like angels upon an almanac singing. Altogether now :

-Thou visiteth the earth/And blesseth it/thou makes it very plenteous-

And now the women sing alone :

-The valleys are clothed/ are clothed with corn/They laugh and shout for joy and the hills drop fatness-

Men alone now :

-They drop upon the dwellings of the wilderness/they drop upon the dwellings of the wilderness-

And the younger girls in front :

-And the little hills rejoice/And the little hills rejoice-

Altogether now :

-Rejoice on every side, rejoice/Rejoice on every side/Rejoice, Rejoice on every side.-

-That will do til tomorrow- says Aunt Becca.

Little children like us have something to say too. Aunt Becca has pinned cartridge paper from our shoulders to our waists . . . faith, hope and charity, and we are to say :

Three crosses stand on Calvary

On one the son of Man I see. . . .

But she did not know about the Baptist church's contribution.

At certain times all churches in the area co-operate . . . Church of England, Baptist, Church of God, Seventh Day and even Mass Mehiah's church . . . for don't we all serve the risen Christ and await the second coming ! This is a day when we thank God and drop our differences. Co-operation is not only in harvest offerings, it is as well in gift of talents.

Our Parson said :

114

-And now we will hear from Harris Ruddock, *Look to Jesus.*-

Miss Trudy who plays for Baptist took the organ stool and played softly tunes we all know but did not sing at our church. She plays *Rescue the perishing, Care for the dying, Jesus is merciful, Jesus will save.* Baba came onto the platform, clean as usual, with his tie erect and jumping from his Adam's apple; his long black socks and his three-quarter pants buckled below the knee-bone. He waited. Miss Trudy starts up *Jesus Saviour Pilot Me* and he begins to speak but soon he isn't there any longer. Nobody saw him. Just the picture he was painting :

> The evening sun was setting
> On a village near the sea
> The uttered benediction
> Touched the people tenderly
> And they hurried to their homes
> As the evening sun was low

> ....
> ....

> Look to Jesus, can you hear
> Look to Jesus, he will save.

He was telling us about a boat that had overturned at sea; that the village people were caught up in the drowning people's plight but they were impotent : they could not swim and had no boats. They only had faith. They could only shout their prayers across to the drowning swimmers :

> Look to Jesus, can you hear
> Look to Jesus, he will save.

I suppose that the people in his story were saved but that was a different matter. Everyone in church that day felt the full measure of his saving power. Saw that power which Miss Sada knew they had. Felt how that power could be moved into saving another drowning swimmer. We did not know when Baba stopped talking. There was only silence. You cannot clap in an Anglican church, but you can cry. Big men had tears rolling down their cheeks.

Aunt Becca closed her eyes and put A-framed fingers across her mouth as if she were keeping a silent prayer from bursting into raucous tabernacle witness. The pressure was too much. She took off her glasses and dabbed her eyes with her little embroidered handkerchief, then began to polish her glasses as if they needed cleaning. Aunt Becca couldn't help it. She cried. With us. Aunt Becca Pinnock, Aunt Khaki had cried from shock. There was something here that she did not need to clean.

JANE AND LOUISA WILL SOON
COME HOME

THE ONE-SIDED DRUM

But I need to be cleansed.

Have you ever seen a new sucker trying to grow out of a rotten banana root? My whole chest was that rotten banana root and there were two suckers. Alexander Richmond knew that I was rotting. I told him to touch me but he wouldn't. Just looked strange and sent me to my mother. I was rotting.

-You are eleven now and soon something strange will happen to you. When it does go and tell your Aunt.- I needed cleansing.

Not all trees let you climb them step by step. Not all trees have branches by their roots. Some trees you have to climb by wrapping your feet around them and hauling yourself up by your chest and your belly. The coconut tree is one such tree. I could no longer climb the coconut tree.

I was strange and everybody knew it. The boys knew it. They kept daring me to hug myself. They knew that I was hard and soft, putty and wood, a rotting trunk and growing suckers. I was not quite alone though, thank God: Janey and Louise were changing too, or so I saw when they came to stay with us that summer when we were eleven. Thank God for that; but it wasn't enough for I was getting much stranger than they and much more rotten. They shared the summer and the hurricane with me, they shared the change with me, but I faced 'it' alone.

We had known that 'it' would come one day but never

thought seriously of, nor discussed its happening to us, though we knew all about its happening to other people. We knew who was having 'it' and who had just had 'it'. We could tell when any of our women folk were about to have 'it'. We knew that when they sat down and made themselves whispers one to the other, they were talking about 'it'. We knew when Sister got 'it'. We were pushed away, she began to do things that had to be done in secret and joined their whisper circle. 'It' was a hidey-hidey thing! It made you a whisper.

It had never happened to Aunt Alice though. She never left us but you see, Aunt Alice was old and never married. She could not make the whisper circle. She had never been like Baba's mother, Cousin B, the whisper circle, like the women. She had no need to push us away. She stayed with us. We didn't want to leave Aunt Alice. We didn't want to be like them and never thought that we would have to be like them. Like those others.

Those others were whispers and echoes. Baba's mother, Cousin B, they were echoes. You heard from them, you heard of them. At times they were nothing but rumours. You saw the doctor's kit and carpenter's tools, the alabaster doll and its lemonade set that they sent but you never saw them. 'It' cut them off from everybody. 'It' spoilt your life if you weren't careful! Yet 'it' gave you power, the power of a duppy that could send presents that nobody else could buy. A hollow duppy with no toes. 'Its' wood ants and termites dug toys and fancy Christmas cards out of you. A chute without dimension, a hollow without name or face, a hollow that pulled innocent girls in, an instrument as hollow and one-sided as a drum, and like a drum, its message reverberated loud and very clear but it carried no physical form nor even image of one. That is you. That's what 'it' makes you.

'It' made me powerful too and in a strange way. 'It' gave me powers over them. I was the centre of attraction. They spent energy to get me clean. Was I taking my hot water baths? Was I learning to wash and cook? Did I remember to wear my rubber-soled shoes to school? I mustn't forget to wear a slip and I must remember to let Aunt Becca know if 'it' came again. I was being given corrupting powers.

'It' corrupted Mass Stanley.

-You getting big Nellie. Hmmmm. Can't see you no more. You leave out the ole man gaan find young man now. But you watch out for the rascal them.-

That hurt for it wasn't true and Mass Stanley knew it and we never did lie to each other. He only wanted to let 'it' come between us. He knew very well that there were no young men. Mass Stanley if nobody else knew, for he watched us carefully when he wasn't thinking things he didn't want to think. We were his life. He knew more than anybody else that Baba and Errol and Barry had gone off to High School and I only saw them on holidays. He knew too that even when I saw them, they didn't see me. Baba never did see me anyway but Barry and Errol had been different. We had been friends. Now they pretended that they didn't see me. Pretended that I didn't know how to catch janga or to play cricket. And when they looked at me, they looked at me strangely. Mass Stanley knew all that so he shouldn't be pretending too.

Only Egbert was still nice and warm. His rolly-polly black pepper hair still smelt of warm wood smoke. He was not in it but his grandfather was. Egbert didn't let 'it' bother him but his grandfather did for him. Now he was always wanting to know what we were doing in the kitchen as if I had not helped his grandson boil hog feeding all my life. He had taken to hearing my mother calling me as soon as I arrived at his house. He let 'it' spoil Egbert for me:

121

-Don't let your father see you doing that with me. I don't able him come talk to me- Egbert had said. That hurt me deep deep down in those places that 'its' erosions had made most tender.

And 'it' came again in all its fullness.

The circle tightened 'round my feet: I must have some dirty un-named thing in me that could make even Egbert dirty.

-She has something in her- they said -Anything could happen to her now. We must ship this one out with the sun. Go eena Kumbla.-

-She had something in her- Aunt Becca said. She had said it too of Baba but in a different way. I have the devil in me and only Aunt Becca knows how to deal with it. I surrendered. I told her. I told her that 'it' had come again and Aunt Khaki used 'it' to seduce me. I have 'it' in me and Aunt Becca Pinnock has no children of her own. I must go to Town with 'it' and her and Teacher Pinnock to his promotion.

The circle narrowed, the distance was complete. Go eena kumbla for you need to be cleaned and preserved like peppers in a kilner jar. Go eena Kumbla. I went with Aunt Becca and the sun.

THE KUMBLA

A kumbla is like a beach ball. It bounces with the sea but never goes down. It is indomitable. Moreso than the beach buoy. The sea never covers it; it never stoops to fight. It takes no orders from the sea but neither does it seek to limit it. The beach ball sets no measures on the sea, seeks not to guide swimmer or non-swimmers; it merely bounces as it will upon the sea, the sand or anywhere. Haughtily.

A kumbla has these properties. It bounces anywhere. Unlike the buoy, it is not tethered. It blows as the wind blows it, if the wind has enough strength to move it : it moves if it is kicked, if it is thrown, if it is nudged . . . if anyone has that much strength, that much energy or that much interest. It makes no demands of you, it cares not one whit for you.

But the kumbla is not just a beach ball. The kumbla is an egg shell, not a chicken's egg or a bird's egg shell. It is the egg of the August worm. It does not crack if it is hit. It is as pliable as sail cloth. Your kumbla will not open unless you rip its seams open. It is a round seamless calabash that protects you without caring.

Your kumbla is a parachute. You, only you, pull the cord to rip its seams. From the inside. For you. Your kumbla is a helicopter, a transparent umbrella, a glassy marble, a comic strip space ship. You can see both in and out. You hear them. They can hear you. They can touch you. You can touch them. But they cannot handle you. And inside is soft carpeted foam, like the womb and with an oxygen tent. Safe, protective time capsule. Fed simply by breathing!

They usually come in white.

Anancy took his son Tucuma to fish in Dryhead's waters.

123

He was taking a chance and Anancy knew it but he didn't intend to starve. Anancy took his son Tucuma to fish but having no skill on water, he rowed right into Dryhead's palace and Dryhead is the king of the water. Anancy went too far this time. He put himself in deep waters. But Anancy is a born liar, a spinner of fine white cocoons, a protector of his children. Not to worry, they'll survive. Anancy is a maker of finely crafted kumblas.

Peeny Wally was in the fishing expedition too but he abandoned them. He had asked Nancy certain questions and had learnt once more that Nancy's eyes couldn't see further than his children: -So is you and Tucuma one fish and is you and Tucuma one going to eat fish. Well me take my light and gone- And he went.

The river was dark. You should have seen it. Good for black hog and they had caught a great number but not good for making your way home when you can't row well, when you have no light and when you are nervous because you are poaching on another man's property. It was dark as mud which begins to assume a life of its own, to form glistening malarial rainbows of light, to give birth to fireflies. Wild cocoes, wild shot, rushes, bhang grass, kept it damp and outside of God's light. Nancy rowed and Tucuma rowed, following this firefly and that:

-Favour like we los' Father-

-Hush your mouth boy, your Father can los' you?-

Anancy rowed and Tucuma rowed.

-Don't follow no firefly boy. Look inside of yourself and row. Them will los' you. Them will put you out of your way. See what nearly happen little while?-

And they rowed.

-But when you find out where you want to go, you watch for them other one what going there and you use their light. See what me do with Peeny Wally? Eh boy? Use his light and don't we have fish? Eh boy? Don't we have fish?

Answer me boy. You ever see so much black hog and janga. Is just left fi wi get home and you know your father never let you down. Answer me boy. True or lie?-

-True sah.-

-So we soon ketch home! Right boy?-

-Right sah.-

-Follow me boy. Now you see like how the night dark and the river like is pure mud, and you see like how them firefly out to fool we. Watch me boy. You see them light over there like is a firefly jamboree. Is there we going. To the king himself. Watch your father boy. Watch your father. Look deep inside yourself, use the senses God give you and learn.-

Firefly is a fire-kitty beast. Jumping up and down all the time. He can give you plenty light but not for Heaven's sake would he stop long enough in one place to do a good job. Jumping up and down like a childish rubber ball, he wouldn't even stay quiet long enough to listen. Well! And an 's' don't mean anything to him at all. Singulars and plurals is the same thing to him for the man would just not listen. And Anancy knew that.

-Come firefly, take this chiles of mine and put him at store house. Things too bad with me. Can't feed myself much less fu go feed five six mouth. Put these chiles at store house man and Dryhead can do anything with them that he likes. He can eat them, he can put them to work. I just can't make it, I pass the point of caring. And I am going to tell him so.- Fire-kitty firefly see children, not child. Put children, not child in the store house and what is more make that report to Dryhead that Brer 'Nancy had come with all his children. Anancy could depend him, that firekitty one!

-Brother Dryhead, you hear my plight. You see how the drought mash me up? I broke, I los', I bow to you. You is King. I just can't make it, can't mek it at all. I bring

125

the children them. All of them. Take them, eat them, work them, anything. I can't manage no more. I just can't make it Brother Dryhead. Things just too hard. Rather than tief, I bring them to you. For your mercy. I wouldn't beg you a thing for myself either, only a bed to rest on for the night.

-See here Brother Dryhead, I telling you. The pickney them give me a hard time to carry them here you see. They know things is hard but we love we one another. You know that 'bout we. So you understand my sorrow. Turn over the boat and try to swim back home I tell you. And I have to get out there in the river and haul them back. So if you smell any fish or anything like that on me, is only that why. I tell you Sir, things hard and my boat, it not even so good. Them punch hole into it and make it worse, for them rather drown than leave them father and I have to take mud and stop it up so that we could get here . . . which reminds me. I going to have to beg you lend me a boat to get back home for my shame tree don't quite dry down yet and I can't force myself as well on you. I know I not asking anything too hard, for you is not like me. You is a big man. You know how to manage and you have plenty boat, can well afford to lend me one.

-I poor but I honest and have mind. I only asking for a bed for tonight and that you lend me a boat tomorrow morning and that through I so tired, you leave it till tomorrow morning before we talk business. Boy, Sir, my children, the children them dirty. Love them you know. Poor children but I have pride (And Nancy cried long eye water). I wouldn't want you to see my children them now. You shoulda see the condition. Maugre and weak but them have pride. Them didn't want to come but I couldn't watch them dead. Pride them have. Them have them father pride. Jump out of the boat. Rather dead than give stranger trouble. Mi poor children and them looking so dirty now. A morning I clean them up and hand them over to you one by one.-

Early next morning, Nancy wake Dryhead.
-Brother Dries. My head not too good you know. Is the pressure. Pressure dey pon mi bad man. Clean forget that your people don't have much use at day time. And I don't want keep your boat. I am a poor man but I honest. Many a man woulda see this as a chance to get something for nothing. I coulda sell this boat to my friend Peeny Wally. He have light better than any two of your men for you know his light steady. And is my friend and he needs a boat and he can buy one. But I could never do that. Rather dead first. Tell you what you do. Lend me one of the children so that he can row me over and take back your boat to you. The biggest one. Send Tucuma. He is the one that understand why I have to give them away. Fact is, me and him talk 'bout it like two big man and he agree so he will bring back the boat. And I beg you, don't eat him. You can't lose off of him. He can work. Now I am going to tidy up the rest of the children and count them off right before your eyes.-

Anancy takes Tucuma out of the store house while the fool-fool firefly who can't see well in the day, just bopping his eyes, seeing doubles and saying :
-Only one at a time. The King say one at a time.-
-See him there. Touch him. Don't you feel say that is only one?-
To Dryhead, big fat and resplendent in his court dress, Anancy says : -See him here Sir, Number one.-

You know how sometimes when you love somebody and you don't want the whole world to know how powerlessly in love you are, you sometimes manhandle him in public.

127

How at the times when your love makes you most vulnerable to attack from outsiders, you scream, kick and curse
the loved one in company? Anancy spoke this kind of
language and knew that Dryhead understood it. His vulner-
ability was supposedly under double attack: he had to ex-
pose his deep love for his children in public and had to
watch himself give away the things that were dearest to his
heart. So it was expected that he would revile them
doubly cruelly at a time such as this. As soon as each
supposed child appeared Anancy would shout at him
contemptuously as he did at this one:

-Your face favour . . . go eena kumbla-

To Dryhead and his court, this was a bad word that
only a man so torn with grief could utter to his child.
To Tucuma, it meant: find yourself a camouflage and get
back into the store house.

-You face favour . . . go eena kumbla-

Tucuma follows his father's command, shrinks as if his
father has insulted him, goes under the cellar as the guard
would have him, changes his colour with mud, crawls
out and around and back into the store house while Nancy
grumbles in a loud voice:

-Time so hard. I try to show you children by reason.
I do all the best I can. I tell you that I have to give you
to Brother Dryhead. He is some of you godfather, he
won't treat you no more badly than he has to, but you
wouldn't even look smart and make him take a fancy
to you. You children going to let me leave with a heavy
heart (And Dryhead was so sorry for him) I wouldn't
do this if I didn't know that is only starvation I have to give
you. Guard see there, is only one I'm taking. Child
straighten your shoulders and go long. Number two Brother
Dryhead. This is the mother's favourite and it grieve me
heart Sir to part with him. . . . Child try to look smart,

fix up yourself, don't shame me . . . you face favour . . .
go eena kumbla-

Tucuma follows the guard, slinks as if he has something
to be ashamed of, changes his colour again, creeps out of
the cellar and around to the back and into the store-room
again in time for Brer Anancy's speech :

-Guard, you sorry for me. Don't it. Talk the truth. To
see a man come down til him have to sell him own pickney.
Feel here is only one. Chile take your father hand. It not
going to be too bad. You will see. Just behave yourself.
Brother Dryhead will love you just like a father. . . . See
him here Brother Dryhead, number three. Chile remember
what your father say. Dry up the eye-water man. Wipe
off your face . . . you face favour . . . go eena kumbla.-

Tucuma follows the guard, slinks as if he is afraid,
changes his colour and rushes back to the store-house. They
do that five times. -See guard, is two here this time. But
you go ask the King if he didn't say that I could take this
big one here with me to row back over the boat. Hold on
to him here. Not this one, the big one, the one on my
right. This big one here is not to go under the cellar. You
feel him up and measure him so that you will know that is
only this said one that is leaving in the boat with me. . . .
Son go back in the corner. Your father soon come for you-

Firefly have no hand so he can't feel nothing but he
don't want Nancy to know what everybody else knows, so
he blinks and would swear blind that he saw two children,
took the measure of the bigger one and saw the other
leaving through the door with Nancy. So Nancy took
Tucuma to be counted by Dryhead for a fifth time :

-Last one Brother Dryhead. Remember you said that
the big boy could come with me and carry back the boat.
. . . Look Brother Dryhead straight in the eye child. Let
him see that your father is poor and that you know that

he has come up on hard times or else he would not be doing you this. Hold up your head man. Smile chile. You face favour . . . go eena kumbla-

Tucuma does what he knows he has to do.

-Guard pass my son here. Let us make the last little trip that we will ever make together. God's willing, he will be a better man than me. Come Tucuma- And they left.

And remember the time when he spirited away all of his children, each into his own kumbla, outwitting the man-eating Tiger? Anancy crafts such finely woven white silk kumblas designed to protect for generations.

But the trouble with the kumbla is the getting out of the kumbla. It is a protective device. If you dwell too long in it, it makes you delicate. Makes you an albino : skin white but not by genes. Vision extra-sensitive to the sun and blurred without spectacles. Baba and Alice urged me out of mine. Weak, thin, tired like a breach baby. Now where are they?

THE SPYING GLASS

Now the spying glass is a totally different affair. You can get in and out of it at will. But it magnifies like a pair of two-way bi-focal spectacles. You see and feel everything twice as acutely. You are seen and are felt twice as acutely. Consider the bind for my tender flesh and eyes after nearly quarter of a century in my kumbla.

-Did you hear what they were saying Nellie? Nellie, I can hear you breathing. I know you are there. If you choose to go around the world getting greyer and greyer and getting stretch marks on your blooming rear. . . . Cho Nellie, don't let me swear.-

-Oh my darling Nellie Gray, they have taken you away and I'll never have you by me anymore. . . .-

-That's a lie and you know it.-

-Know what?-

-You are in one piece. You are together again. As much as anybody else at least . . . don't forget, you can be seen clearly now. You cannot get away with lies.-

-Well then . . . why did Aunt Khaki want to clean me?-

-That's not quite fair.-

-Remember I too can see clearly now. Why did Aunt Khaki want to clean me?-

-Did you hear what they said Nellie?-

-They whom?-

-You know whom. Did you hear what they said?-

-"They did their part"-

-So?-

-So what? Who's asking the questions around here?-

-Who said "why did Aunt Khaki want to clean me?"-

131

-And if I did?-

-What did they say Nellie?-

-"We did our part"-

-So why did Aunt Khaki want to clean you?-

-She did her part-

-You had better believe it-

All those squares, all that washing and never finding their whiteness. Poor bleeding heart. Poor Aunt Becca. It was pitiful.

-Nellie, I can't stand tears. Self pity wastes time especially when it parades as feelings for others. You can be clearly seen Nellie-

-All right Aunt Alice, you needn't leave-

Aunt Alice Whiting, great grandfather Will's daughter who never married but spent her time visiting, helping out here and there . . . Aunt Alice took out her projector again as if the true purpose of life was to show films. It was a lantern slide this time:

Here is Rebecca Pinnock, nee Richmond. Look at her face. See how she throws her head back. She is proud. Here is her house. What is it made of? Wattle and daub. Does Rebecca Richmond look like wattle and daub? No she does not. Here is a house. What is it made of? Spanish walls, bricks, shingles. Does it look more like Rebecca Pinnock nee Richmond? Of course, it does. Who's is that house? Rebecca's grandfather Will's . . . my father.

Why does she not live in it? Why does she not live in it Nellie? Because her mother fell. You've listened at enough key holes to know that. You know that. Because her mother fell. Fell for the wrong man. He married her. Don't worry. She started a long line of legal marriages. But who was he? Look at him Nellie. At your grandfather. Nice, gentle, kind, black pattoo without a red cent to his name. Look at your

132

grandmother, Aunt Becca's mother, my sister, an angel, almost unblemished skin. You know the lesson Nellie. Keep your head screwed on. If you don't, a nice gentle pattoo might get it. They didn't get mine. More is the pity.

And you now Miss . . . the scratches on your rear have healed. Get up and walk. At least your Aunt Becca did. She broke her leg yes, here and there but what of it? Use your heart Miss Nellie. You have heart. Look now at Rebecca Pinnock. Who plays in her hair Nellie? Who pulls out her chair Nellie? Nobody. Does she have young ones Nellie? None at all. But she is married so how come?

She is barren. Threw away Tanny's child and made herself a mule. Lived through his hatred . . . but you know that. Suffered Pinnock who suffered her because of what you call her khaki. But is she home? Is she at peace? Only half-way back to dear grandfather Will and his brick house with its shingled roof. Only half-way home. Spinning in purgatory, her soul, her heart and her baby are in thatched huts, perspiration and drums, praying for peace. You remember . . . why is Aunt Becca praying in Mass Mehiah's church? So who is going to call her out of her cocoon and put back her heart and her body together and her baby in her arms? Wake up Nellie. She tried. Its your time now and I can take you no further.-

With that, Aunt Alice who never married but spent her time visiting and helping out here and there, stuffed her projector in its case and left with one teasing glance in her age-old flirtation :

-The moving camera next time. Beware. But in any case . . . Jane and Louisa will soon come home.-

133

THE MOVING CAMERA

Name this child
William Alexander Whiting

It was a baby corn light yellow morning when William Alexander was christened. A baby girl had been crowned queen. A monarch but a woman. One doubted her wisdom but never her kindliness. A true queen. For all her kind heart, those heathens had got uppity! Already lazy, they had taken to putting on airs, putting up houses and refusing to do their rightful work in sugar cane . . . and were being rightly hanged for it. Those non-conforming, trouble making friends of apes . . . ! The world was getting brittle, cracking when queenly kindness was rewarded thus. The world was cracking and this little reddish yellow bundle was doing nothing to hold it together again.

As red as his red-necked poor-white parents, he represented lines and generations of the watering down of the stock. Still this was one more white to correct the one to ten skew. But did it have to be a poor white? This kid wouldn't even put a comma to the world. Howsoever that may be, my job is to make him a child of God, a member of Christ and an inheritor of the Kingdom of Heaven and to do this to the best of my ability.

Albert and Elizabeth Whiting did not see it quite that way. This was their first fruit, chubby and as intelligent as a number eleven mango with a purpose. His purpose was to help them take another step towards their rightful place. And as for poor . . . as far as they knew, they were far better off than many others and far better off than their fathers. Tobacco was not exactly multiplying like locusts but please God, they were growing. They were nowhere near the rectory nor the big house but they could see them and while this little lad lived, anything could happen. The four-roomed brick and shingle house had not always been four and it still had space for expansion to accommodate this little boy and his brothers, for them to put up servants quarters and the like and to expand perhaps with time into a great house. There was space, there was time and there were hands of newly displaced blacks. With time, this little chap would spread himself in the sun.

William Alexander yelled to that. He acknowledged his membership in the Anglican communion and into the faith of his fathers. He acknowledged that the parson had done his job well but his divinations: they were limited and he wished he could tell him so. So were those of his parents; but hush don't tell them yet. William Alexander sensed that neither the insipid parson nor his doting reddish-yellow parents knew that he was to be the hope, the blanket, the kumbla and calabash of a black dynasty.

And after William Alexander, there were nine more and for every child, Beauty made a playmate so that Albert was getting the reputation of being an up and coming cattle man as well as a tobacco man. He could feed his family with milk and meat and rent oxen to the mills and turn their labour immediately into cloth, steel, iron and all the other things which his hand and his land could not yield. He was fast becoming big massa, hirer of labour, lender of money, powerful miller to the little colony of hillside blacks seeking to grow their way out of their thatched cottages and into the soil. The great house was round the corner! But success was too sweet for Elizabeth: she died with the eleventh.

Madam Faith, the kindly blue-black Nanny kept the house going. There was nothing else going between Albert

135

and her. Before God and man, there was nothing else going. But it was still a pity that it had to be her in the house. It was a pity that there were so few white women around and so few who would hire themselves out to an up and coming red-neck family. True there were fine upright spinsters but they wanted marriage and Albert was not about to share his heart again, was loathe to fill Elizabeth's side of the bed again and in any case eleven children was quite enough. Better the kindly old negress. So you see there was nothing untoward going between Madam Faith and he as far as he could see. But you know Albert was never much of a diviner.

He couldn't, wouldn't touch her body nor she his but he gave her his problems and she gave him her counsel and she knew how much of everything he had, where it was, what was going wrong with what, what was flourishing, what was floundering and so on. And he gave her his children. She knew who was given to lying, who was susceptible to colds, who liked fried plantains, who would grow to be a tall lad, who liked his back massaged and who distrusted those who touched his head. Madam Faith was part of the family, all of her except her body and we do not know how that would have gone, if dysentery had not taken Albert away and left her in charge of his eleven red-necked children.

Madam Faith taught William Alexander how to be a man and how to carry on the affairs of his father's house. And nobody should criticise her if he became a colourless man, if he loved her goddy Tia Maria and saw no evil in it, if she turned her back while William Alexander's manhood strengthened itself in her pride. And after one time, is two time, until that couple were formed like cement spouting khaki children.

William and Tia were not just fruitful and vigorous

lovers: they were fruitful and vigorous workers as well.
Everything they touched multiplied. Their steps were in
tune: she worked foot to foot with him deticking cows.
She could replace any of the hands in the tobacco gang;
she could argue the price of a cow like a man. William
was a happy sinner. When God called, he merely put the
receiver to a deaf ear; when a few inquisitive high-minded
souls asked questions, he maintained the silence of a brick
wall. A sinner he was but not a faithless one; he kept his
promise to his father to see his brothers into trades and so
he did until the house was empty of the very last one. Then
Tia settled in to make a better life for her khaki children
and why not? A baby queen was getting fat and old, a
township close by had been sacked, a Jew had found his
way at court, and black people had got uppity enough in
this land to maul and kick a custos to death . . . things
could change so why not?

Why not indeed?

Tia could not tell you whose womb had pushed her out
into the sunlight but that did not matter: she knew herself
to be a lucky little girl who had missed the slavery days by
a hair's breadth. And that was enough to be proud of.
Madam Faith's belly did not know baby pains but a mother
is not the one who groans but the one who cares: she
was a good Nanny, knew how to take a baby and how
to take care of one so she was a mother. It was only left
to God to put a child of her own into her hands and Tia
came: god mother and god daughter. She taught her the
mysteries of the property, the ins and outs of the business,
how to make soup, how to stretch it, who was to be feared,
whose bark was worse than whose bite. She knew she had
trained her well enough to carry on a white man's business
but she never dreamed that luck would carry her and her

137

children into his house. Life was complete; Madam Faith could fade away and she stepped boldly out of the picture.

But though men have killed a white custos, they do not expect to see a black one in his place; and though men have sired khaki children, and left bequests to them, they do not expect to see them playing on their father's knees. William was an abstract being, subsequently stretched through time and shades of colour. He was a man of a brick wall: he could not see, he could not hear. William was like the universe: he moved by no clearly observable path. He moved but nothing that you could see moved him. When a man is blind, what need has he of a sergeant major's baton? A horse knows the way home because he smells it. William's one perennial ailment was hayfever and he lived among cows and hay so there was no way he was going to smell anything. William was a diviner. He could read the future as he had at his christening but the vibrations of his immediate surroundings were totally lost on him. He was an abstract being, living in his head and his family and totally unaware of other tunes and innuendos.

Not so with Tia: she had her eye-sight and Madam Faith had impressed upon her the importance of clean ears. She had no respiratory ailments so there is no way that she could not feel the absence of a clear-cut path. Two roads lay before her: none was kind. There were his people and there were her people and she knew who had power. Love, luck and strength were not enough. She'd have to learn to bob and weave. And Tia started to weave one of those purely spun kumblas, growing out of the top of her head and billowing under her feet somewhat like a bridal ensemble. She nurtured one in each of her children:

-You mustn't say bway, you must say bai. Talk like your father.-

She didn't know the drum and very soon she did not know what a nine night was. My poor great grand Tia!

138

She was a national laughing stock . . . "girl is smell you want to smell like Tia Maria, find your place". She overdid things a bit! But William never saw.

Great grand Tia did everything to annihilate herself . . . her skin, her dress, her smell . . .the oodles of perfume. She malapropped before Miss Malaprop was popular. Yet the cows multiplied and the tobacco grew more verdantly than before and her children got taken into the highest schools. In truth, the more she denied herself, the more the things around her grew. The lesson was clear: the path was becoming clearer: the things she loved would prosper in inverse ratio to her disappearance. Tia wanted it so that with a snap of her fingers she could disappear and her children would loom large in their place in the sun. The stranger the words her children spoke, the happier she felt. The fewer their experiences she could share, the more progress they had made. The more they turned their backs on her, the more her smile widened into the classic cheshire grin. The more their kumblas billowed out and hardened into white steel helmets separating her from each and each from each, the more peacefully she rested, the more sure she was that they had found their places in the established world to which William belonged, a world that was foreign to her, a world that was safe and successful.

But nurturing a kumbla is like nurturing any vaccine, any culture. Some skins react positively, some don't. Kitty's didn't. My pretty grandmother Kitty's didn't. She liked the music, not of the piano, but of the drums, of tramping feet, steel drums and bamboo fifes. She loved the clear bell echoes of the hammer on iron, of the tinkle of tongs of a non-descript blacksmith/sawyer. She liked to hear the echo of the axe against a tree, his whipsaw cutting wood: and Tia Maria drew herself up to the blackest depths of her anger and banished her. She had shamed

139

her father's blood. But great grandfather Will, blind as ever, found nothing wrong with visiting her in her thatched tattoo, with taking her children on his knees and with giving her what gifts the pride of her pattoo husband would allow her to take. Great grandfather Will was a colourless man with natural blinders.

It was not that Puppa Richmond my grandfather hated himself or anything. It was not that he wished to deface himself or any such thing why we have heard so little about him. Great grandfather Will had been kind to him but that was not all. He plain and simply liked and respected the man and so his name became in his household, a household word, synonymous with good, kind, intelligent, christian. He taught his children to return the old man's love, allowed his wife to cook and wash for him when Tia found the ultimate course of self-renunciation, when the old man's children had abandoned home to find their places in the sun and when it had become crystal clear that little Alice was not quite right in the head and would never be able to keep house. Puppa, a naturally humble and thanks-giving man would even have moved over to give the old man and Alice space in his house but when he chose to live by himself, he did the next best thing . . . he sent his son Alexander, named for him, to keep his company. Puppa did not intend to make great grandfather Will a god to his children : he liked the man, was grateful for his acceptance, saw his need and saw it as his duty to help him especially as he could not help but know that his support of him had lost him the use of his wife. No, he did not intend to make him a god; he did not intend to make him more than he felt him to be — a kindly man — but for want of an alternative romance, great grandfather Will became established in his line as the embodiment of all that was good and desirable.

It is not true either that Tia Maria left great grandfather

140

and squandered his money on another man. She left him yes, but not in a physical but a spiritual sense for the poor woman went clear out of her mind when Kitty got pregnant and chose to marry the Pattoo. Good needs bad to make it look better and the distortions of poor Tia's life story was a good enough mask for the fact that great grandfather Will had no business head at all and that when Tia Maria in the onrush of her madness refused to cipher for him unless he was willing to abandon the viper and her tribe, his business crashed, the bottom fell completely out and he had no idea where it had fallen. Nor is it true that great grandfather Will had had a great house and that his children were tricked out of it and out of all his remaining money by his brothers. What is true, is that William had not married Tia, had not made a will, had not protected his children's interests and the brothers took what was lawfully theirs. Great grandfather Will willed us nothing but his abstract self and what cocoons we could make out of it.

THE PILL

When a body senses pain or danger or uncertainty, it seeks
protection. Some smoke tobacco, some take pills, some lie
on dreams. When a thing successfully protects, it becomes
your talisman, a part of your personal culture. When it is
used by many others and they begin to believe in its powers,
it becomes a part of the way of life of the group and they
make for it whenever the need arises. Some people need
protection more than others and use the thing more often
and in larger doses than others. But everyone shares the
value of its usefulness and the necessity to use it. Tia Maria
in the prime of her life, had built a fine and effective kumbla
out of William's skin. She willed us its protection and even
those who did not know her or had not heard of her,
acknowledged the presence and potency of this talisman.
Aunt Becca's need for protection seemed greatest; nobody seemed to mind that she used it most. And Aunt
Becca is not a selfish woman; she showed me where to find
and how to wear my kumbla . . . "those people will drag
you down child. You have to be careful of them".

She had seen her cousins rise then fall. Letitia, Teena,
B. Black sperms disintegrating black wombs, making hollow
women and name-less pointless children. Hadn't she seen
her mother's fall and spawning poverty? Wasn't she old
enough to have felt the warmth of the brick and shingles
of Great grandfather Will's house and to feel the difference
in thatch in cold December rain? Black tinged woman, if
you manage to hold your head up at all, you should freeze
yourself in that position and wait to be lifted as the earth
turns. Do not turn around on your own momentum; if you

142

do so, you will fall. "Woman luck at dungle heap, fowl come scratch it up" but in the life of a black-spermed woman, it is a miracle that finds the right cock. So freeze yourself and wait and how better to wait than in the shade of a kumbla? So build yourself one if you haven't got one but if you have a tried and trusted one, why not use it?

So the black womb is a maw. Disinfect its fruits with fine sterilised white lint if you can. You suck a wasp's sting from a child's hand, clear its nose of the bluish green blockage and spit. The black womb sucks grief and anger and shame but it does not spit. It absorbs them into its body. Take an antidote. Silence it. Best pretend it doesn't exist. Give it a cap of darkness, take a pill.

So it had been for us. With every orgasm, a white lie must be born, an image, a cowl, a kumbla to cover its fruits. And even with the cunning of the kumbla, the game was lost: it was the womb or its fruits. So Tia had to die that her children could live. Aunt Becca had to kill hers so that she could live, and cousins Letitia, Teena and B had simply dropped U-roy and Locksely and Obadiah and vanished in the crowd. What a life! What an abominable scrap heap thing is this thing womb.

-That's no gift love, even if we did need gifts. That's something you throw on a scrap heap- He spoke their words for them. So this was what Baba knew and was trying to steer me past. Aunt Becca had said he was sent here for a purpose.

So you must sit still like an alabaster baby in your kumbla lest you be your Cousin B. You must wait to move as the earth moves and the sea turns; as the wind blows as he who cares and has enough strength to, kicks your kumbla?

So why was Aunt Becca still looking for her baby in thatched huts, bamboo benches and drum meetings? Poor

143

thing. She had left her heart outside her kumbla and it was as naked and as pitiful as my body now scarred and scabbed by the revolutions of the spying glass. Aunt Becca had not stood still. In spite of all her warnings, she had not stood still : she was still searching for a way to put the body, heart and womb together without risking complete annihilation. She was still hoping to make it real. She did her part eh Aunt Alice. Blessings on mine.

THE FISH

I do not know whether my mother's people needed that
kind of protection. I do not know them. Granny Tucker is
all we had and I do not know whether she did. I only
know that she prayed. I do not know if prayer is a kumbla.
I did not peep at her nor live with her. I do not know
whether she wrapped herself in prayers and flew away at
times from the troubles of this world. I know that she
always knew things and through her Jane and Louise knew
too. I really do not know how Granny Tucker managed
but Jane and Louise would soon come home and they
would know.

It happened that they did not know. They had peeped
and listened but never saw nor heard her with a man.
They had heard her talking and laughing, fighting, teasing,
cajoling, flirting with God and her Corpie but they had
never ever heard them return her sallies. Fact is, nobody
seemed to know her Corpie but her. My mother did not
know him. She had been born after his time and God,
well. . . .

In her later days Janey and Lou had seen her shadow
boxing, they said, her wiry black hands clutched into fists.
She was not ready yet, they said she kept saying. Old Israel
wouldn't let them touch her thigh! Just clutched her fists
and bucked the air like the Old Lady at Papine. Must
have been trying to hold her head up high on her limbering
black neck for that was what she told them in the end:
-Hold your heads up high, use your hands. It is your life,
live it.- That's all she gave them by way of a blessing.

No. They did not know. They couldn't say for they had

never ever seen her with a man. They could not even say whether a blessing was a kumbla or a prayer a kumbla for Granny didn't talk to them much. Just prayed. They knew though that they were tired of holding their heads up high, scrubbing their hands to the bone and dragging around life on their bottoms like Sirhie, the bitch, in the hope of keeping male dogs at bay.

They had hands and a bottom though. They could sit. That was something. Soon I should be able to sit too, to hold up my head high and to use my two hands.

We lived in a mossy covert dim and dark and we could make it even darker when we played dolly house in our sink hole searching for treasure or when we stared into the irridescent black ink that made our nights. We were familiar with the dark, very familiar. Tia Maria had burnt her skin and bones and left us a thick felt hat of darkness, her negatives and her strong sense of smell. We didn't need light. She had given us the whites of great grandfather Will's eyes.

Ever see a fowl sitting on eggs in the cold December rain? We knew the warmth and security of those eggs in the dark of her bottom. Til Mass Mehiah cut down his bastard cedar trees and let the sun in.

Vulnerable as a premature worm, we returned . . . the place still lovely with coconut trees and fine banana trees shifting their shoulders like rag effigies of our politicians, like dying swans, dancing with quiet controlled conviction, trees growing out of our kin planted in the soil. Trouble was, fat water grass had over-run our paths. No paths lay before us. We would have to make them.

But we still had Granny Tucker's wiry black hands, strong enough to scrub away khaki suds so why not to pull water grass. Not much else had changed: the smell

146

of the air and the feeling of hope were still there. Madam Faith still tied the bankside and the Tia Maria, the white coffee flower still perfumed our garden. Mass Nega mine yourself. We are cleaning our garden. Mass Nega, wi smell you dinner but wi no want none. We are crawling around your pits and shelters low on our bellies for we still have bellies, that organ which sheaths and protects but gives forth fruit. Crawling strengthens its muscles and dragging on the ground in time gives it its own camouflage. With luck we will grow feet and stand, then perhaps Baba could come out of the light bulb, Cock Robin could stand up and sing again and the man on the lonely donkey needn't dissipate into smoke.

We are getting ready Aunt Alice.

Mass Nega mine yourself. Mi smell you dinner but mi no want none. We walk not by your leave or in your shade but with your blessing.
where it became a square gold fish bowl with one fish parrot fish, so large that it stretched my belly to the point
Last night I dreamt I was carrying a fish, a large sized

stuck crossways in it. I could touch the tail where the nurse had prepared me but no amount of bearing down could give birth to it. Strangely enough, I felt neither sadness nor frustration nor even pain that the fish couldn't come for afterall I could still see it.

It will come.

Goodbye great grandfather Will, Tia, Granny Tucker, Corpie, aunts and uncles and cousins.

Goodbye Aunt Becca.

We are getting ready.